The Trouble with Maggie

A tale of heroism, hedonism,

hankie-panki, and hocus-pocus.

Gillian Long

With special thanks to Liz for her advice.

The Trouble with Maggie

By Gillian Long

First published in 2016.
Millaa House Publishing
PO Box 89
Millaa Millaa
Queensland 4886
Australia

Cover Art
John Russell

ISBN-13:978-0-9942671-8-4

Millaa House Publishing

Contents

1.

Sydney 1995.

Maggie lies in a pool of urine, listening to the twins' scream. A phone rings incessantly behind the teller's counter and Maggie wishes someone would pick it up. It's driving her crazy. A film of dust covers the floor which smells of dirt and disinfectant. That's something she hadn't noticed when she walked into the bank.

The booted weight of the gunman is still heavy on her back, pinning her to the floor, but it makes no difference, her limbs are frozen by fear.

Will it hurt if he shoots her? He might shoot her in the head. Perhaps shock takes over, and she'll feel nothing. It'll be over before she realises. Just so long as the twins are all right. They won't remember, and kids are resilient.

Her captor shouts, 'kill that bastard phone,' and a burst of automatic fire blows it, and the desk to shrapnel.

The noise frightens her babies' and their cries become more demanding. Paul whimpers as Abigail's scream rises in tempo. In response, milk gushes from both Maggie's breasts. It soaks the remaining dry spots on the front of her clothing. After a moment's lull the howls become louder.

The agony of listening to their screams is unbearable, and she blocks it out, focussing on practicalities. If she dies, Joe will be a good father to them. Will he find someone to replace her? The thought of evil step-mothers pops into her mind. Perhaps it's better for them to go with her.

Guilt batters Maggie's brain. It's the first time in the twins' short lives she has not responded to their cries, but she's immobile under the man's weight and her own terror. She can't think of them now. If she remembers the details, she might yet find a way to survive. Focus Maggie, focus. If she can recall everything since the premonition, perhaps it will give her clues that will save her babies.

It was less than an hour ago she stepped out from the small semi she and Joe rented? She pushed last night's forebodings aside as she felt the effects of spring. Perhaps that was her first mistake. Yes, she sees it now. The sun shining, a few clouds scuttling by, driven by a sea breeze and she convinced herself that Joe was right. She was imagining things. Best of all, the winter rain had gone.

She strolled towards the bank to withdraw money for their planned lunch date. It's her twenty-first, and Joe promised to meet her in the park for fish and chips. It's not much, but with the twins and Joe's meagre salary as a tutor, it's all they can manage. Still it was to be a treat away from the humdrum of motherhood

She sucked in the briny air to blow away any lingering dread and quickened her pace. Her thick wheat coloured ponytail bobbed with each stride. The ancient double seater pram clanked and rattled along the pavement. At each join in the concrete she did a little skip. Bad luck befalls those who tread on the cracks.

Along the street, roses and azaleas spilled over the fences of tiny front yards, or nestled against sun drenched walls. Blossoms perfumed the air as bustling bees packed saddlebags with pollen. Magnolias, bare of leaves, struggled to prop up branches heavy with waxy pink blooms, Maggie's favourites. She stopped for a minute to gaze around her, wondering why she let last night's gremlins ruin her birthday. With spring's beauty in full display, it's hard to remember the premonition clearly.

This morning she had awoken in a lather of terror, her dream fuzzy, but still clinging to the edges of her mind. She lay stiff under the blankets, listening to Joe breathing until the sun rose, telling herself nothing lurked under the bed. Ghosts and demons don't exist.

Or, that's what Joe said anyway although she's not convinced. When he stirred, she rolled closer, hoping he would cuddle her. Usually, he stumbles to the shower, hardly speaking until after his first cup of coffee.

'Hold me Joe, I'm scared.'

He cleared his throat. 'Of what?'

But his arms went around her, and his erection pressed against her hip.

Afterwards he said, 'happy birthday,' and kissed her nose, noticing her worried frown. 'It was just a nightmare, honey.'

'It felt like a premonition, as if my grandmother was warning me of something.'

He laughed. 'Premonitions only exist in fiction, babe. Sometimes when you wake up in the middle of a nightmare, it can leave an emotional imprint hanging over you, like the sword of Damocles.'

'The sword of what?' His dismissal hurt, but she tried to hide it. He hates it when she complains that he doesn't understand her. It's better to say nothing, but she wishes she was as clever as he is.

'You know; the story about Damocles desperate to become king, but not wanting the responsibility.'

'I don't get it.'

'Yes, perhaps it was a bad analogy. What I was trying to say is, when you wake up after a nightmare, it leaves an emotional imprint that might account for your fear.' He pulled away.

'Stay a minute, please Joe.'

'Come on honey, I have to shower or I'll be late for work.'

Abigail woke and wailed, setting off her brother, and after that Maggie had no time to think. She fed and changed the twins, got Joe's breakfast, and waved him goodbye as he cycled off to work, but the feeling remained. It loomed over her like a dark shadow, its ill-defined edges oozing evil, and she knew it was more than a dream.

Once she stepped into the sunshine she convinced herself Joe was right. He usually is, banging on about how rational thinking is so important. That was her second mistake and then she had compounded it by stomping on the next crack with both feet, doing a little swivel and grind, as if to say, there! It hadn't lasted because she immediately fell back into avoiding the cracks. She couldn't help it, but the damage was already done.

She would never admit her secret. Joe would laugh, with that look of disbelief on his face as he searched her features to see if she was joking. He's always saying there is only science. All else, religion, superstition – everything, disintegrates under scientific scrutiny. It's hard to argue. She doesn't have his education, but every day she sees evidence of the supernatural world. It's enough to convince her, and now lying on the dirty black and white tiled floor of the bank, she has all the proof she needs.

All she ever wanted was to be a good wife and mother; to have Joe's love and respect and raise well-adjusted children, but she's failed. If she had listened to her grandmother's warning, instead of her husband, they wouldn't be here now. She doesn't need a university degree to tell her that.

How she wishes she had been content to stay at home rather than hankering for more excitement, but instead she had to push onto the bank. How silly she was as she fussed over the lack of a ramp as she hauled the pushchair up the first step.

That was when the man strode across the pavement. He shifted his sports bag strap on his shoulder and took the lower bar of the pram. Maggie bit her lip, trying to quell nervousness about stranger danger near her babies. After all, he was being chivalrous.

He nodded, his brown eyes appraising, his hair greying at the temples. The grey made him look distinguished, and trustworthy. Joe might look like that when he's in his thirties although Joe's eyes are serious with light and dark splotches of grey, like a thunder head.

The man walked ahead of her, towards the bank entrance. He was her third mistake. Instead of paying attention to the clues her grandmother threw at her, she watched him, admiring the nice long curve from broad shoulders to narrow waist. He'd make a good dancer, lithe and alert, with muscled legs and a tight bum, thrusting against the confines of his jeans.

Instead of heeding the warning she had let nostalgia for the academy flood through her. She wouldn't swap her family, not even for a career as a dancer. She told herself, the chances of her making it were negligible. There were so many talented people, all ready to cut the next person's throat to get a chance in a chorus line, and she never had the singular ambition required.

The man held the door, scrutinising her as she passed. She had wondered if he was flirting. How stupid that seems now, but it was so nice to think she might be attractive, now that all her femininity seemed swamped under piles of soggy nappies, milk-drenched tee-shirts, and mushy baby-brained synapses. What an idiot. How could she have missed it?

'Thanks,' she crinkled her nose. The man should wear deodorant if he wants to be taken seriously. That's another thing Joe thinks is weird. He calls her passion for tidiness and hygiene quirky. She knows he means obsessive, but if she wasn't, she wouldn't know what the gunman looked like, and in hindsight it was another clue she had ignored.

Her mind recalls the interior of the bank as she walked through the door. The teller's queue was already eight deep. A young man, dressed in a leather jacket and blue jeans, stood at the counter. He turned his head and Maggie had been struck by his looks. Dark hair, square jaw with a trace of shadow, masculine shoulders and narrow hips. It made him look classically beautiful although he might have preferred handsome. He couldn't be more than eighteen, a few years younger than her, but more confident as he withdrew the last of his savings, telling the teller it was for a plane ticket to Queensland.

She can't see him now. Not that she can see much at all lying face down on the floor. The old woman, who she thought looked like her Gran except for the foot encased in plaster, is blocking her line of sight. Oh how stupid she is. That was another clue. The woman's husband lies next to her, his eyes screwed shut, and she wonders why the men didn't do something when the gunman grabbed her?

Maggie tries to recall who else was in the bank. In the queue behind the handsome man was a mother with her teenage daughter. They waited in silence as the daughter, dressed in mini kilt and Doc Marten's picked the varnish off her fingernails, dropping each flake to the floor. Beneath her lashes, she had stolen glances at the handsome man, but either he didn't notice or he ignored her.

It was ridiculous in light of her current predicament, but Maggie had hoped her twins would never be as self-absorbed as the girl. Now she just wants them to survive, and they can be as egocentric as they please. The couple behind the girl watched the varnish flakes drifting to the floor, and the woman had rolled her eyes at her husband, nodding in Ms Doc Marten's direction. Her husband smiled, seeming more tolerant.

It was such a small thing, and so inconsequential, like Maggie fussing to position the pram in a shaft of sunlight falling through a high window so the babies would stay warm. She noticed a tradesman in blue overalls had glanced at her, but looked away when he saw the pram. It happened a lot lately, and she wondered if she was becoming invisible. If only she was. Could that also have been a clue, a reminder to make herself disappear?

Behind the Tradie, an older man in his fifties, wearing expensive jeans, had talked loudly into a mobile phone. He's silent now. Why doesn't he use his dumb phone to call for help? Maggie shifts her head and sees his boat shoes and ankles poking out his trousers. He has no socks. What a Bogan.

She hadn't understood what was happening when the hand grabbed her pony tail, and wrenched her backwards into a hard body, choking off her scream as an arm clamped around her throat. Metal pressed against her temple, as the robber shouted, 'nobody move or she gets it.'

She had scrabbled against his forearms as her vision narrowed. Darkness descended to leave only a tunnel of light. She couldn't turn her head, but she could smell him. It was the man who helped her up the stairs.

'On the floor, the lot o'you.' He waved a pistol.

The customers fell to the ground, except the old woman who no longer looked anything like Maggie's grandmother.

He had yelled, 'you too old hag. Flat on your belly now, eyes down.'

The old woman struggled to her knees and onto her belly, letting her cane clatter to the floor. Her husband covered her hand with his. Outside, the sun slipped behind a cloud, switching off its shards of light, casting the room in gloom.

Maggie's legs sagged beneath her, and the man relaxed the choke hold around her throat. Blood thumped back through her temples. From her peripheral vision she could see another man, shorter and stockier than her captor, his face covered by a black balaclava.

His voice, singsong with lack of concern, said 'ladies and gentlemen, this is a robbery. Everyone stay calm, and no one will get hurt. You,' he pointed his sawn-off shotgun at the nearest teller, 'open the door.'

Another man, with the wiry build of a labourer, dressed in black tee-shirt, and tweed Balmoral cap, the kind English gentlemen wear for shooting parties, danced through the opened door. Under the cap, his face was covered by a black bandana, painted to look like a muzzle-full of canine teeth. The front of his black tee-shirt was painted with a howling Jackal, underneath which Maggie noticed the artist's signature in large looping letters.

Despite his disguise, he looked older than the other two men, and Maggie saw grey hair poking out from the base of the cap. Over his shoulder, he carried an army camouflage printed bag, and in his right hand an AK 47, which he pointed at the teller. 'You know the drill mate, fill 'er up.'

Paul whimpered. The man holding Maggie adjusted his grip to swivel his body to watch his comrades, and Maggie wrenched herself away to tend to her baby, but the gunman was there before her. The click of the safety catch was loud in the hushed silence as he pressed the barrel against Abigail's tiny blonde head.

'No!' Maggie cried and fell to her knees

Abigail wailed.

'Shut the fuck up,' the man with the shotgun shouted across the room.

Her captor said, 'try that stunt again and your ankle biters are raspberry jam.' His voice had a foreign lilt, but the over tones were Sydney, like he had lived there a long time.

Maggie knelt next to the pram, head bowed, 'sorry—sorry. I won't do anything.' She glanced up at him. A balaclava covered his face, but in his brown eyes she saw her recognition of him reflected.

'Don't look at me bitch. Get down on the floor and don't move.' He leaned closer to speak in her ear. 'Identify me, and you

8

and your sprogs are dead. I'll find you wherever you are, no matter how long it takes. I'll hunt you down, and I'll enjoy gutting them while you watch.'

'Please, please, I'll do whatever you want... Please.' She slid onto her belly, lying in a pool of warm liquid. It seeped through her dress wetting her stomach, but she was shaking too much to notice. The gunman's foot settled on her back, weighing her down as she listened to her babies' cries.

Her captor shouts at the other two robbers. 'Come on, hurry it up.'

Then the booted weight lifts from her back. The door opens, and they are gone. Maggie scrambles to her feet. 'My babies,' she sobs, 'sorry, so sorry.' She soothes Abigail with a dummy in her mouth, and strokes Paul's cheek.

The handsome man in the leather jacket bolts out the door after the robbers. A burst of rapid fire splinters concrete around his feet, and he ducks back inside the doorway. He returns to the counter and writes something on a deposit slip.

The old woman pulls herself up and hobbles over to help Maggie. 'Are you all right dear?'

Maggie rocks the babies with her hands on their little bodies. Abigail sucks; her small brow wrinkled in fury and then calms. Paul whimpers, but quietens as his sister settles.

'They'll be all right dear,' says the old woman.

A high pitched voice from behind Maggie says, 'oh gross. She's peed herself.'

The handsome man looks at Maggie with compassion in his blue eyes. He takes off his leather jacket and drapes it around her shoulders. A police siren wails, and Maggie bursts into tears.

2.

Queensland, October 2013.

Maggie watches Belinda Zonda go through her dance moves. The nine-year-old has a cloud of dark hair framing a pale oval face, and blue eyes fringed with dark lashes. She's graceful too, but she will never achieve her goal to become a ballet dancer. She's too tall. Not that it matters, and Maggie won't dash her dreams. Ballet is good exercise, and the girl will fit into the class nicely; time to speak with her father.

Maggie looks out the window to the hotel across the road where he said he would wait. Two Bikies pull up outside the hotel. Perhaps she will wait, in the hope they'll be gone soon. She smiles at the girl. 'Let's try the barre, Belinda.'

The hotel is like many North Queensland pubs, built in the early 1900s. Large wrap around verandas, with white painted fretwork, squat under a tin roof. Multiple French doors lead out onto concrete pavements beneath bold letters boasting the hotel's name.

Inside, high ceilings, with elaborate pressed metal panels, grace a utilitarian bar with a wooden counter running its length. Gaming machines flash in the corner, their tinkling music merging with the soporific lullaby of beer fridges rumbling, and a television mumbling.

Dog-eared advertising leaflets, pinned to the walls with blue-tack, offer specials on Rum and Coke with a bag of Pork Scratching's. They jostle for attention alongside old black and white photos of pioneers clearing the rain forest.

Rough-hewn fencing poles section off the far end, with a sign saying lounge. Peeling coffee tables and battered armchairs crowd the space, and another sign advertises coffee, tea, and scones with apricot jam and cream.

Three men lean against a high table, watching the television in silence, occasionally lifting beer to their mouths. A fourth man sits in the lounge reading a newspaper, his back to the wall, a cup of coffee on the table before him.

A barmaid sits on a stool behind the bar, flicking through the pages of a magazine. She's pretty, a little plump, in her mid-thirties and sceptical about life, but it's the only life she knows. She lifts her hand to wave away a blow fly, but otherwise skims through a magazine article asking, *do you have a skinny kitchen?* Now and then, she glances up from the pages to see if the man in the lounge is still there. It's a long time since she last saw anyone that hot and wishes he would look up from his newspaper so she could catch his eye.

The growl of Harley Davidson's makes her turn her head. It's a sound she doesn't hear much since they brought in the new bikie laws. They have New South Wales number plates, but must know about the law because their plain black leather jackets have no patches. She relaxes. She doesn't want more trouble.

Brendan O'Riley and Taylor Blunt leave their bikes parked in the street and walk in through the open French doors. The sour smell of last night's spilt grog greets them, but it's familiar and better than the lingering smells of vomit and piss that haven't been adequately hosed off the hot pavement.

O'Riley leans on the bar, one foot resting on the rail as he scans the beers on offer. 'Give me a middy of that.' He points at one of three beer handles.

'We call it a pot darl. Middy tells me you blokes are from south of the border.' She smiles, showing a missing canine.

Brendan scowls at the wooden counter. Taylor scans the faces in the bar, but recognises no one. It's his first trip to Queensland, but you never know where your fellow inmates end up, and it's always better to check. He looks at the barmaid wondering if she's worth staying here for the night, but decides it would be a mistake. She's too old and would be desperate and clingy.

She picks up a glass, her brow arching as she mimes the question, *same for you?* Taylor nods, and she takes another glass. While she pulls the beers she tries again to make conversation. 'You're not from around here then?'

O'Riley ignores her. She slides a beer across the counter towards him and pulls a second. O'Riley takes a long pull and wipes his mouth.

Taylor steps up to the counter and after glancing to see if O'Riley will answer, he turns back to the woman. 'No, just visiting, passing through actually, on our way to Cairns.' He hands her a fifty dollar note.

As she walks to the till, she says, 'oh yeah, visiting the reef?'

Taylor watches the flesh at the top of her arms wobble as she dips into the drawer for change. He is suddenly revolted by the dimples of coagulating cellulite and looks away.

O'Riley makes a hawking noise in his throat and Taylor frowns. Bad behaviour before you understand the lay of the land can cause trouble. 'Excuse my mate, he's Irish.'

She smiles. 'We get plenty of Irish gentlemen in here. Tourist like yourselves, visiting the reef. Most of them's got manners, but.'

She uses the North Queensland vernacular at the end of her sentence which confuses Taylor. He wonders, but what? Before he can ask, another man comes into the bar and sits on a stool nearby.

'Give us a schooner Trish love.'

'Look at you Raffy. I nearly didn't recognise you without your jacket and patches.'

Raffy frowns and gazes out the door. His fingers drum a tattoo on the wooden counter top. 'Ah shit,' he says as a police car parks next to the bikes. 'Fucking grunters. What do they want ruining a bloke's pint?'

She looks at him in alarm. 'You haven't gone and done something Raff?'

'No Trish. I'm clean. Looks like they're interested in them bikes.' He nods at Taylor. 'Those yours?'

The man in the lounge lowers his newspaper. He takes in the situation and raises his paper again, but continues listening.

Taylor jerks his head at Brendan and gets up to look out the door. One of the police officers strolls back to his vehicle and climbs into the cab. The other saunters around the bikes and looks up as Taylor leans against the doorjamb.

'Yours?' The police officer asks.

Taylor nods. 'Yes mate. Got a problem?'

The officer shakes his head and walks back to his partner.

Taylor goes back into the pub. In a low voice he says to O'Riley. 'I don't like this Bren, let's go.'

O'Riley frowns. 'Finish your beer. We have a right to be here. We aren't doing anything illegal.'

Taylor's eyes flick around the room. 'I have a bad feeling.'

Brendan says, 'oh, so it's a bad feeling now is it? You're always telling me I'm superstitious. Now it's you who has bad feelings, and I must act? Hey, but when it's me as says something isn't right, you mock.'

Taylor glances at the barmaid. Now is not the time for an argument. 'Mate, we should just go.'

'When I've finished m'beer. I'm not budging for no one 'till I'm done.' He picks up his pot and takes a long draught, then opens his mouth to release a yawing burp.'

Another police car pulls up, and two more officers get out. The four Police walk into the pub.

An officer with three chevrons on his sleeve says, 'haven't

you boys heard of the new laws?' He hooks his thumbs into his belt and rises on his toes before rocking back to his heels. 'Here we have three members of a criminal gang, fraternising in a public place.'

'Bullshit!' Raffy stands. 'Give us a break Macca. I don't even know these blokes.'

'Yeah Macca,' Trish says, 'they're tourists. This one's Irish,' she points at O'Riley.

'Sorry boys. The law's the law. You'll come along quietly now.'

'Shit!' Taylor looks around for a way out, but there's nothing. 'Shit, shit, shit.'

Brendan looks bewildered as the police officers usher the men towards the exit doors.

As Macca reaches the door he glances across to the lounge and stops. His eyes squint, and then with a nod to a constable, he says, 'give me a minute.' and walks over to the lounge area.

'Chris Zonda, I thought I recognised you. I heard you had transferred to these parts. Are you working, or do you live in the village?'

Chris raises his steady blue gaze to Ted MacDonald. 'How are you Macca?'

'Doing my duty. What about you?'

'Day off, just passing the time.'

'I heard about your wife. Terrible thing—commiserations mate.'

Chris's eyes cloud. 'Thanks, it was a long time ago.'

'Look, I cook a mean barbeque if you want to come over sometime—meet the boys.'

'Thanks. I'm just settling in.'

'I heard you have a little girl. How old?'

Chris's features transform as a slow smile spreads across his face. 'She's nine. I'm just waiting for her.' He nods to the town hall across the road. 'She's at a dance lesson.'

'Ah, with our very own Miss Maggie.' Macca winks.

Chris frowns and looks at his paper.

Macca glances out the window. 'Well, I'd better go. Got me some crap to clean off the streets. Good seeing you mate. Give us a ring if you want company.'

Five minutes later, Maggie walks into the lounge with Belinda. Trish waves her tea towel.

The child says, 'there he is.' She smiles up at Maggie, and points at Chris.'

Maggie says, 'Go on then. I'll be with you in a minute.' She walks to the bar. 'What was that all about?'

'Ah, you know these crazy bikie laws. Poor old Raffy, but they'll have to let him go. He didn't know those blokes. He'll be right.' She drops her voice and leans across the counter. 'Who's the hunk? He's drop dead gorgeous.'

Maggie shakes her head. Trish is insatiable. She changes the subject. 'When's the next meeting?'

'Fifteenth, can you make it this time?'

Maggie says, 'I don't know Trish. The twins will be home. I'll ring you.'

Trish nods in Chris's direction. 'Come on. Who is he?'

Maggie shrugs. 'They just moved into the village. He wants to enrol his daughter in classes.'

'Well when you've finished with him, send him my way.' Trish winks.

Maggie winces and turns away. As she approaches Chris and Belinda, he stands and ruffles his daughter's hair. 'How was it?'

The little girl's eyes shine. 'It was awesome.'

Chris glances down, amused at his daughter's enthusiasm then looks back to Maggie. 'So what's the verdict?'

'Of course; she can join the intermediary class.' Maggie smiles at Belinda, 'she has talent.' She holds up a sheaf of papers. 'I'll need you to fill in forms and get your details for insurance. The council insists.'

'Can I buy you a coffee, and I'll do it now.'

Maggie glances at her watch. 'Okay, thanks.'

Chris examines Maggie's face. 'You look familiar, have we met?'

She laughs. 'I doubt it. Where are you from?'

'Sydney, but I was in Townsville for a few years before I transferred to Cairns a couple of months ago. We've just moved up to the village to get out of the heat.'

'Oh, I come from Townsville. Well, I was born there, and spent parts of my childhood there although we moved about a bit. Mum and Dad still live there; or rather they have moved to Magnetic Island since Dad retired.'

'Really,' Chris looks surprised. 'Your Dad isn't Stan Fraser by any chance?'

It's Maggie's turn to be surprised. 'You know my Dad?'

'He was my station sergeant when I came out of basic training; must be almost eighteen years ago. Good bloke.'

He grins, and Maggie's stomach constricts. She hands him the papers and says, 'sorry I have to go. Maybe a raincheck. Bye Belinda, see you next week.' She touches the girls shoulder and rushes out of the pub, her cheeks burning.

Chris gazes after her puzzled by her sudden departure. He's certain he seen her somewhere. It'll come to him. 'Ready for home, Bindi-boo?'

3.

November 2013

Maggie leans her elbows on the kitchen bench to gaze out the window. She loves this view with its green stretch of cattle-dotted paddocks fringed by rainforest, and the backdrop of mountains rolling away into the distance. It's so peaceful, so remote, and so safe, but most importantly, its 2,600 kilometres from Sydney.

She straightens her back, and smooths a stray length of hair from her face, adjusting the plastic Alice band she uses to keep it out of her eyes. Although she looks young and vulnerable for a woman of thirty-nine, years of constant anxiety have etched lingering sadness into her eyes.

She knows she shouldn't have stayed after dance class again to see Belinda's father. When she met with him last week she told herself it was just to collect the paperwork and make sure he didn't think she was weird rushing off when they first met. So, there was no excuse for staying on today, but she feels an affinity she can't explain. It's like they knew each other in a previous life. Still, she worries people will gossip if they see her sitting with him in the pub. Even though she knows it is just a harmless coffee with one of her pupil's parents, someone will misconstrue her motivation. Today was the last time.

She tucks her hair behind her ears, pushing Chris from her mind to worry about the twins. Tomorrow, they'll be home from university for the Christmas holidays. Somehow, she made it through their first year away, but she won't be happy until they are here on the farm, safe in her care.

After they left, she had nightmares for weeks. Joe said it was empty nest syndrome, but he's wrong. Her anxiety is not for her own loneliness although she knows she is lonely. It's for her twin's safety. It's always about them, but Joe just doesn't get it.

Thank God for Trish. At least she understands. She grasps the amulet around her neck and turns back to the pot bubbling on the stove. The garage door slams; Joe's home early. That's a surprise. He's been getting home later and later lately, with all the extra work he has on his plate, but she's given up complaining.

A minute later he walks into the kitchen. 'I'm starving. What's for dinner? Do I smell curry?'

'You're home early.'

'I'm officially on leave for four whole weeks.' He walks up behind her and peers over her shoulder, grimacing as he looks into the pot. 'Is that our dinner?'

She laughs, 'no silly. I'm making shampoo. It has fenugreek and curry leaves—good for your scalp, no nasty chemicals. Trish says that's why your hair's thinning.'

He looks hurt and touches the top of his head. 'Thinning! It's not thinning. It's a fine head of hair.'

Maggie turns, appraising her husband with her head tilted at an angle. 'Hmm, no its not, and you are always scratching. Trish says that's because you are allergic to the additives they put in shampoo. She gave me this recipe.' She opens a jar of salt and takes out a good pinch which she rubs in her hands.

Joe watches her with an exaggerated frown.

Maggie glances at his face. 'Salt gets rid of the smell of garlic.'

'You put garlic in it?' His voice climbs an octave. 'Surely you don't expect me to use that gloop in my hair. I'll smell like downtown Calcutta. Jesus, I can imagine the nicknames the students will give me if I turn up at campus with that stuff in my hair. Or do I rub it with salt to get rid of the smell?'

'Don't be daft.' She swallows her irritation and tries a more conciliatory tone. 'Just try it okay, and see if it makes a difference.

You can do it while you are on leave.'

'If I go to Magnetic Island tomorrow with that stuff in my hair, your Dad won't let me on his boat.' He tilts his head, mouth pursed. 'On the other hand, maybe that's a good thing. He doesn't think much of my fishing prowess at the best of times.'

'You're not supposed to be fishing. We're taking the twins whale watching.'

'Huh, your Dad will fish until we find a whale to watch.'

'He'll have plenty of time to fish later. That's why he retired there.' Maggie sighs. 'Poor Mum.'

Joe's worried. He knows what Maggie's mother is like. 'Mags, I want to be back by Sunday night, okay. I have a meeting in Cairns on Monday. Don't let's make plans to stay longer. I know your mother will try to guilt us into staying.'

'How come you have a meeting? I thought you were on leave.'

Joe shrugs and looks away. 'My publisher wants to go over the chapter outlines of my book.'

'That's good, isn't it?' Maggie lifts the pot from the stove. 'Budge out the way then. This gloop is ready for bottling.'

'How long before dinner?'

'Don't know. I haven't started it yet. Why?'

'I might go and shower and pack for tomorrow.'

'I packed already. Just a weekender, but you can see if I missed anything. The suitcase is open on the bed.'

'Okay, I'll just shower then. If you haven't started cooking yet, can we have Bali curry? That smell made my stomach rumble.'

'Okay if you get a chicken from the freezer while I bottle this.'

Joe walks out the kitchen and along a corridor towards the garage where they keep the deep freezers.

Maggie calls after him. 'Oh and Joe, can you see if there's any coriander?'

He returns with frozen chicken thighs and a bunch of coriander from the garden. 'That trunk of my folks' is still cluttering up the garage. I might go through it this holiday.'

'Okay.' Maggie looks at him carefully. She knows Max and Beth's deaths were a shock, especially coming so close, one after the other, but it was nearly eighteen years ago. Every few years, he opens the trunk with good intensions, and takes out one or two articles then puts them back. He never says anything, but Maggie knows he can't face it. Perhaps he really will do something this time, but she doubts it. 'Can I help?'

'Maybe.'

Maggie doesn't know why he's so reluctant to go through it. If it were her parent's stuff she would be desperate to see what was in there as quickly as possible, but Joe has always been funny about his folks, his dad particularly.

She suspects they never really got on, but she's never been able to winkle more than a few bare facts from him, except that his father took every opportunity to belittle him. Even in the card he left to her and the twins in the will. The last time she asked Joe about his father, he said, 'I didn't really know him that well. He would come home after I went to bed, and often be gone before I got up. On the weekends he was either in his shed, making things or out with his mates. I hardly saw him, and when I did, he would seldom speak other than to give orders. Mum said he suffered depression from the war, PTSD I guess.'

He slides the chicken onto the bench. The packet's iced bottom skids across the counter, knocking the open salt pot onto the floor.

'Whoops.' He pulls an apologetic face. 'Sorry. I'll get a broom.'

Maggie holds up her hand. 'No wait.' She bends to the floor, takes a handful of salt, and dribbles some over her left shoulder. Then she reaches out to do the same for him. He jerks away as she releases it.

'Jesus Maggie. It was an accident.'

'Well…' She turns away.

'I said I was sorry.' Joe glares and shakes his shirt to get the salt from under his collar.

She fidgets and looks at the ground. 'Spilt salt is bad luck.'

'Ah, not more of Trish's bullshit. I don't know why you listen to the witch.'

Anger bubbles up before she can stop it. 'You say witch like it's a bad thing. Everyone knows about spilt salt. It wasn't Trish who taught me that.'

'Who then?'

'My Mum.'

'You're all barmy.'

Joe stomps off to have a shower. He's given up trying to get his wife to reason logically. In the bedroom, he takes his phone out and checks the messages. A text from Lexi asks if he wants to meet for a drink before he heads home. The phone has no signal. It never does on the farm, but he taps out a response anyway. With any luck a text might slip through on a stray microwave. He glances around then re-reads the message before he hits send. Sorry I missed you. I left early today. See you Monday.

He shouldn't be doing this, but he can't help himself. He just wants to sit and chat—that's all. She has such an intriguing mind; so intellectually stimulating as she talks about music. He's been starved of it for so long. Surely just talking is okay. She's just a friend and colleague. A voice in his head says, 'so, if she's just a friend, why don't you want Maggie knowing about her?' He shakes his head, puts down his phone, and opens the en-suite door to go and shower.

An hour later, dinner sits on the cooker keeping warm. The aroma of garlic, galangal, chopped coriander, chilli and coconut milk fills the kitchen as Joe returns. He sniffs in appreciation and dips a spoon into the creamy sauce. The irritation he felt at his wife's superstitions has faded.

Maggie walks in through the back door holding two eggs in her hand. 'Lazy chooks, only two eggs.' She catches him scooping curry into his mouth. 'Joe! Tch,' she sucks her tongue from the roof of her mouth.

He puts on his little-boy-guilty look and says, 'it's a brilliant afternoon. Do you want a glass of wine on the terrace before dinner; celebrate the start of my leave?'

'Sure. You go. I'll just put the eggs in the fridge and be out in a tick.' The phone rings and Maggie answers. 'Hello. Oh Julian, hi. I'll call Joe.'

Joe pulls a face as he takes the phone. He doesn't much like the American exchange student, but the bloke did offer to take care of the place while they are away. He should be more grateful.

'Julian. Well done on completing your dissertation.'

Maggie puts the eggs away. The fridge is almost empty, with just enough for Julian's meals over the weekend. She makes a mental note to go shopping on Monday and takes out a bottle of wine before grabbing a beer for Joe. Then she wanders out to the veranda leaving Joe talking to Julian.

He's a lovely young man, so handsome and well-mannered in his rich American way although she is a bit worried about Trish's behaviour towards him. He's almost young enough to be her son, yet you wouldn't believe the way the two of them carried on last month at the golf club.

Maggie sighs as she sits at the outdoor table and takes a sip of wine. Neither of them are married, and they are both consenting adults, so why not. Trish accused her of being jealous. But she's not, is she? After all, she has Joe, and she loves him, no matter how irritating he is sometimes. She's an ungrateful woman hankering after more.

4.

The Shedding of Innocence

The following morning, an hour before dawn, Maggie wakes with a start. Remnant terror from a dream fills her mind. It's been years since she last dreamed it. She thought she was cured, but its back. She fumbles for the amulet at her throat, and remains stiff under the covers, afraid to move.

Outside a swishing noise washes back and forth across the window pane. It's only leaves blowing in the wind. She scans the room, but she can't see anything, just the darkness pressing against her eyeballs. Shadows shift and shimmer as she strains to hear another sound. Which shapes shouldn't be there?

The descending whistles of hunting owls scream in the distance and a dingo's howl drifts up from the valley. No. It's only her imagination. Nothing is amiss. She wants to wake Joe for comfort, but he'll just be annoyed with her.

She mouths an incantation for protection, and questions whether by drawing patterns of evil energy into her dream state, she isn't manifesting its creation. Was the dream an omen or precognition? They say dreams can warn you of impending danger. Is danger already here and her mind is acting to alert her, or is her grandmother trying to warn her of things yet to come? Trish will know what it means.

Maggie lies on her back, her breath shallow, eyes staring into the dark, as she works out what she should do. The hour passes and dawn breaks above the mountains, its grey light creeping through the uncovered windows. Once her mind is made up, she feels easier, shuffling lingering foreboding to the corners of her mind. Growing certainty calms her. If she stays home everyone will be safe. As if to affirm her decision, a morning sea breeze

24

ruffles the open curtains. Chimes tinkle and refracted light from hanging crystals, casts kaleidoscope colours around the room.

Joe stirs next to her and rolls onto his back, his eyes screwed into slits against the growing light.

She wonders how he will react when she gives him the news. Perhaps she should fake illness. In a low voice she says, 'Joe, I can't go.'

'What?' He clears his throat and sits, his legs crossed under the cover.

'I just can't go with you, to pick up the twins.' Her voice wavers, and she pulls up the cover to hide her face. 'You'll have to go by yourself. We can go whale watching another time.'

Joe squeezes his lower lip between his thumb and forefinger. His brow furrows as his gaze focuses on the forested peaks in the distance. 'Why?' He drags the word into two syllables and waits.

'Tch...' Maggie clicks her tongue. 'Because... well, nothing. I'm not feeling very well.'

'What's wrong? How unwell?' His hand rubs the back of his neck.

'I didn't sleep.'

'Oh.' He releases his breath. 'Is that all? You can kip in the car on the way.'

'Can't you go? Please. I'll stay here. You'll be home by tonight. Or you can stay at Mum and Dad's and come home tomorrow or the next day, like we planned—take the twins to spot whales without me. The kids will be disappointed if they don't go out in Dad's new boat, and I'll only get sea sick anyway. Mum will like it if you stay.'

Bewildered, Joe stares at the hump in the bed. 'We planned the trip months ago. You can't back out now, not because you're a bit tired.' He inhales to calm himself, but he feels his pulse racing. The older she gets the more irrational she becomes.

Maggie prevaricates knowing he's angry, but how can she explain? Even if she tries, he will refuse to understand, and there'll be a row. The silence drags on, accompanied by the rhythmic pulse of his fingers picking the knots of the Celtic design on the bedspread.

The fear returns, swelling in her mind, filling her with dread. Travelling today is like giving the finger to fate. She did that last time, and it changed her life forever. It doesn't matter how cranky he gets, she can't surrender. 'Please.'

He coughs and clears his throat. 'I thought you were looking forward to it. Geez Mags…' he sighs, 'ditching our plans is not an option—not now, not at this late stage, and you can't seriously expect me to go to your folks without you.'

Maggie knows she has no choice. She must give him a reason and tries honesty to test his reaction.

'I can't—it's too dangerous.' She pulls the cover down to reveal pleading eyes, hoping to deflect his fury.

'What?' Joe clears his throat. His forehead creases to vertical furrows, and his voice catches. 'You're kidding! What's too dangerous?'

'Me going.'

'But it's your parents. Where's the danger in that?'

'No, it isn't them—it's…'

'You're not making sense.'

'I don't know, I… it's not specific.'

'Yes, you do.' Joe is beginning to recognise the problem. 'It's some ombie goomby superstition again, isn't it?'

'It's a dream.'

'Ah ha! A nightmare?' He can understand that; so long as it's not more shit that mad moll, Trish concocted.

'Yes, I suppose so.' She searches his face for sympathy. 'Oh Joe, I'm scared. It's another premonition. I know it.'

Joe stretches his jaw, relieving the tightness. It's just a nightmare. Perhaps he can dispel her qualms with reason. 'Maggie,' he pats her shoulder, and represses the sarcasm welling in his throat. 'My lovely Maggie... you know nightmares are not premonitions, don't you?'

Maggie wrenches the covers over her head, coughing into the bedspread to muffle her words. 'Patronising bastard!'

'Pardon, I didn't catch that.' The tightness in his jaw returns, and he yawns again. 'Maggie, I'm trying to help.'

'Leave it Joe, just leave it.'

He fingers his lip, wondering how he can help her see the nightmare in a rational light. Logic calms him. 'You know Maggie,' Joe fixes his focus on the remote mountain peak outside the window. 'I read a theory that dreams are the mind's way of sorting and filing memories for retrieval. They are rather like a clearing house, a way of tidying the mind.'

He glances down at her under the covers, but she's silent so he ploughs on, searching for a metaphor. 'You see, dreams are like librarians, putting away books in your mind. Your dream sorts and categorises your day's experiences and files them for easy retrieval.'

He pauses, reviewing the sentence, and nods, patting her shoulder. 'Your day's experiences, thoughts and sensory input are like books. During the day, they crowd your mind, all higgledy piggledy. At night, the unconscious mind sorts the masses of information, filing it in the right places. It causes information to zoom around your synapses to settle in the right spot, like a book finding its alphabetical order. Of course with all that sensory activity firing in your brain, your conscious mind...' he looks down at her, expecting a challenge. 'You are conscious even when you are asleep you know?' She doesn't react, so he continues. 'Well your conscious mind tries to make sense of the activity, and so it creates a convenient story line.'

Maggie exposes her eyes and nose. 'What are you talking about? What do librarians have to do with anything? You know Joseph you can be a bit strange sometimes.' She turns away, retreating beneath the covers.

'No hang on, the librarian is a metaphor. Oh hell, never mind.' He gives up and tries to overcome his irritation. 'What was your nightmare about?'

'If I tell you, you'll say it's a lot of gibberish,' Maggie's voice muffles.

He breathes in, trying to maintain patience. 'Well you have to admit...'

'You see, I haven't even told you, and I can see by the look on your face.'

'You can't see my face.'

He draws back the bedspread and leans over to give her a conciliatory kiss. She jerks the cover, and the sharp edge catches the outer corner of his eyelid.

'Shit Mags.' He leans back against the headboard rubbing the edge of his eye.

Unaware of what she's done, she says, 'I don't need to see your face. I can sense it. You talk a lot of drivel; reading rubbish about dreams being librarians who sort books. It's okay for you to talk nonsense so long as you say the word theory in front of it, but when I... Oh never mind.' Maggie realises she has gone too far. She doesn't want another row.

'No come on. What does that mean? What are you trying to say?' Joe concentrates on the silken knots of the bedspread. He hates the Celtic design. The thing looks like a Christmas tree. He much preferred her muted French provincial phase.

Maggie sits up in bed, knees to her chest, clutching the sheet to her chin. 'Well okay then, mister clever trousers. How come your librarian theory is better than my theory of premonitions? You always tell me that what can't be measured, can't exist. How do you measure dreams which sort sensory input? That's just fantasy. Dreams are not librarians. They don't sort things. They are stories and images, not facts and statistics. They do have meaning though; real meaning, for real people, who have dreams with real experiences and real emotions.'

His fingers begin again, plucking the knots on the bedspread.

'Oh Joe stop it. I know you hate it, but you needn't ruin it.'

He puts his hands under the bedcovers. 'Real people? Dead people you mean.' His voice rises and he coughs. The conversation has gone off track.

Maggie tucks her hair behind her ears and says, 'obviously dead people don't dream, but I'll ignore that. I was talking about people who are alive.'

'What? You make contact with living people through séances.'

'Sometimes, I think you act dense deliberately Joe. We only contact the dead through séances. Living people dream. Sometimes the dead can cross over through the dream world and pass messages to us. I read about such premonitions. One person I read about in America dreamed her grandmother told her to stay away from short fair-haired men. So she did. She fled from every one she encountered, and you know what? It turned out that the serial killer stalking the town was short and fair-haired. Her grandmother saved her. I also read about people being told how to cure themselves of diseases.' The scepticism in his face makes her wild. 'Yeah, even cancer...'

A pulse hammers in his throat. 'Huh, that's the nub. They just make up the stories to sell you stuff, Maggie. It's the snake-oil of charlatans.'

'It's not... They don't. Their stories are real. They care, and at least they appreciate people. They can see the value of feelings and have respect. Not always trying to be who they aren't.' She bites her lip in belated restraint.

'What's that supposed to mean?'

Maggie jerks up the covers. 'Nothing, I don't want to argue.'

'No, say it'. His lips compress in a tight line.

Maggie steers the conversation away from his career. 'You read rubbish about librarians in a magazine and say it's true, but when I read about healing properties of natural medicine, you scoff. Trish says...'

'That mad leso! You're not seriously telling me...'

'She's not a lesbian.' Maggie throws off the covers and swings her legs over the side of the bed. 'I keep telling you, she's a free spirit. She says women should not shackle themselves to just one man.'

'Huh, probably because she eats them up and spits them out for breakfast.'

'Joe, that's mean. Trish is lovely, and she's kind to me.'

Joe thinks that's debatable, but keeps the thought to himself.

Maggie continues. 'Anyway, Trish told me about a woman who lives near here, and cured herself of cancer...'

'What, using that stuff you call Magic Healing Balm?' Joe rolls his eyes in disbelief at Maggie's gullibility.

'Yes, MHB cures people of all sorts of things. I read the evidence, the eyewitness accounts, and the science behind the balm. There have been miraculous cures.'

'Oh Maggie, that's not science, that's mumbo jumbo. The word magic should give you a clue.'

Defensiveness turns to resentment. How dare he treat her like some kind of simpleton, talking down to her as if she is three years old? 'Oh mister PhD doctor of ants. What good is it, knowing about ants? At least these people cure human illness. They care.

30

They don't drone on about insects for a book that will never be published!'

'It's not... I don't... insects, entomology and...' Joe sighs. 'Oh, never mind, it's hopeless.' He retreats to where the conversation began. 'So you're not going to bother to pick up your own children?'

'Don't! That's unfair.'

'You're happy to make me go. You think that's fair? You expect me to drive all the way to Townsville to pick up the twins—and then I suppose, I just turn around and come back home—do I? Forget the holiday. No fishing, no whale spotting, no swimming, is that what you want?'

'That's not fair. It's not what I want, but I don't have a choice. You can take the kids fishing with Dad. I don't want to ruin everyone's holiday, and I'll be all right by myself, so long as I can stay home.'

Joe stares at her for a moment, wondering if the depression has returned. It's no use arguing when she's like this. Instead, he tries to make her rethink her position by talking about the consequences. 'We'll have to ring the kids and your parents and give them the bad news. They were looking forward to it. I suppose you want me to do that as well?' It doesn't work.

Maggie shrugs. 'Well don't start talking to them about dreams being librarians. We don't want everyone to think you're mad.' She giggles, and skips into the en-suite bathroom.

Joe slides down the bed, dragging the covers around his shoulders against the morning chill. He doesn't feel like doing anything if they aren't going to Magnetic Island. He thinks of the eight hour round trip to Townsville, chauffeur-duty, and closes his eyes.

Lexi's face swims into focus as she smiles and touches his wrist, thanking him for reading her journal article on the

Juxtaposition and clash of musical idioms used in different countries' film making.

Last night he dreamed about her, saw again the exciting glimpses of flesh as she leaned provocatively across to get her paper. He fantasises about her bent over his desk, of the primeval wash of lust flooding through his veins, of the mindless, adrenalin-fuelled thrust against her firm round bottom.

Joe wipes his lips. He knows its fantasy. He loves Maggie, despite being irritated by her weird beliefs. He doesn't even know Lexi very well, but she's intoxicating, and his secret, which makes him feel alive and terrified at the same time. At least his dreams aren't subject to Maggie's daft interpretations or veiled criticism. His hands slide down his body. The noise of the door opening stops him and he opens his eyes.

Maggie stands at the bathroom door.

'Come back to bed.' He pats the vacant space beside him.

Rejecting the clear intention of his invitation she says, 'I'm going to shower.'

He stares at the ceiling and calls out. 'Do I really have to go and pick up the kids by myself?' There is no answer, and he throws off the covers to get out of bed, muttering, 'this is the limit, no holiday, no sex, just chores and responsibility, endlessly until I die, while she gives her attention to ghosts and those weird friends of hers. Bloody lesbians the lot of them.'

She opens the door again, but if she heard him she gives no sign. 'You go. It'll be all right for you. You'll have a good time with the kids and Dad. Mum will be really cranky if none of us turn up, and it's only me who can't go. The premonition is about me, not anyone else. I'm sure of that much because I read our stars yesterday, and I should stay close to home. Yours and the twin's horoscopes are good too.'

He ignores her, and stands in front of the window gazing out across the paddocks, the dream's erotica still impacting on his body.

'Oh Joe, I wish you would wear p.j's to bed or put on a dressing gown. What if someone sees you, walking around naked like that?'

'What someone? We're miles away from our nearest neighbour. Who's going to see me?'

'What if we have a burglary?' She chews her lip. She doesn't know why she said that, but his obvious virile nakedness makes her anxious.

'Out here, are you nuts? What poor desperate prick is game enough to choose this remote spot to burgle a house without any good booty?'

She ignores him, unamused at the intended pun.

He tries again, 'I suppose I could poke him in the eye.' He looks down at his erect penis.

She tries a different approach. 'What if the house caught fire and you had no clothes on when the fire truck arrived?'

'I'll risk it.' Joe gives up. 'I like sleeping naked.' He sits down on the side of the bed, thinking this is the nearest thing to sex he's likely to see today. Refracted colours catch his eye as a breeze sets crystals jangling. God, he hates this whole new age bullshit.

Maggie closes the bathroom door. She feels rejected and resentful. Joe just doesn't understand. To him it's all about sex, but she wants romance and passion; wants to feel appreciated and admired. She stares at her reflection in the vanity mirror. He thinks he is so much cleverer than she is, and he's so selfish.

She pulls her nightgown over her head and examines her naked breasts in the mirror. Saggy! They wouldn't drop a pencil now. Perhaps she should get cosmetic surgery. That's what Trish said she would do if she had enough money, but where do you stop? A lift of the breast; then what, tighten the flabby upper arms? She puts her fists in the air, elbows bent, showing her muscles.

That's better. She will have to walk around like this all the time. The thought makes her giggle, and she strikes a pose, smiling at her reflection. 'Atlas, holding-up the world.' Crow's-feet crinkle around her eyes. She pulls the skin of her face straight. If she followed Cher's example and got a complete makeover— top to toe surgery, she would look twenty again. That would make Joe sit up and take notice. She'll start at her head and work down, until her breasts, bottom, the dimples in the top of her legs, every bit of skin, will be ironed-out smooth. What happens to all the excess?

Maggie turns away from the mirror, and pulls her thick bobbed-blonde hair away from her face, tying it in a ponytail. Perhaps if she pulls the ponytail tight enough, it will smooth the lines. She turns on the taps in the shower, wondering if she is past it, wondering where her youthful beauty has gone, yearning to feel cherished.

What will happen to her if anything happens to Joe? Will she still be able to attract another man? An image of Chris Zonda flashes in her mind, and she shakes her head. No, she doesn't want another man, even one as ridiculously handsome as he is; only Joe, but she needs to know if these things are possible. She's forty next birthday, and all she can see ahead of her is more of the same.

Has Joe gone off her? Lately, he's always irritated. Sometimes, she thinks he puts up with her from habit, or even fear of stepping into the unknown. It would be nice to see him look at her with respect or even admiration, occasionally. The way he did before when he first met her. The way Chris looks at her, with that intense blue gaze, like he's really interested in what she has to say.

Trish says she's wasting her life in humility and servitude to just one man and flaunts her own stream of one-night stands. Joe says it's because she can't get them to stick around, and Maggie wonders if that's true. Is she happy with her way of life?

Sometimes she envies Trish's freedom, but she also pities her loneliness. At least she doesn't have the constant worry and fear for her family's safety. With that thought, Maggie's anxiety returns, and she says a prayer of protection for her children. That's the best thing about her friendship with Trish and the other women in the coven, now she has learned how to ward off evil.

Joe knocks. 'What are you doing in there, brewing spells?' His voice mocks her through the door. 'Hurry up, I need to get in.'

Maggie pokes out her tongue at the closed door and walks into the shower. 'Use the other bathroom.'
'Pass my soap bag then.'

5.

Hubris

Joe steps out of the shower and turns on a transistor radio. As he dries himself, he stares at his reflection in the mirror, wondering if he can get away without shaving. A man of forty-four years gazes back. Lines of time and sun crinkle the skin around his eyes. Sallow cheek planes narrow towards a firm jaw, covered with the dark shadow of twelve hour growth. At least his beard's not yet grey. He stretches his neck, checking for jowls, but his chin is still firm, and he runs his hand over his chest and down to his stomach, feeling the hard plane.

Maggie's behaviour worries him. The flat refusal to pick up the twins is weird, even for her. A premonition; what the hell is that about? He wonders if he should speak to someone about his wife's tenuous grip on reality. The last time she saw a counsellor, she blamed her anxiety on her husband, saying Trish was more helpful in overcoming her depression.

The counsellor told Joe not to worry. It would pass. He called it *the empty nest syndrome*. Maggie refused to see him again saying, the bloke was a closed minded quack who knew nothing about her. Joe can't see how an irrational belief in the paranormal is open-minded.

He sighs, wondering what he might do when he gets back from Townsville. The rest of the weekend stretches before him with nothing planned. Perhaps he will go fishing off coral bombs with Stan although he should finish the last chapters of the book.

The publishers have been threatening to pull the plug on the deal. He'll have to phone and speak with them on Monday to keep up a semblance of truth about having a meeting with them in Cairns. He promised to have coffee with Lexi and go over the score she wrote. She wants Joe to perform it with her at the Civic Theatre, and he's tempted. It's been a long time since he played to a real audience, and she makes him realise how much he misses it.

Perhaps he should start playing publically. Perhaps he could get a gig in an orchestra for a start. He has contacts, but that would require he moves to the city. Maggie would never agree to that. Why she insisted on moving to this backwater in the first place is still a mystery although he can't say he's sorry. The only things he misses about Sydney are live music venues and the opera. He doesn't miss the traffic.

He sighs. Perhaps he will make a start on finishing the book when he gets back from Townsville. Or, what the hell, he might stay down there for the weekend. Despite what he said about Stan not thinking much of his fishing expertise, Joe was looking forward to it.

A resident tree frog, hiding under the lip of the toilet bowl, gives a loud croak. The sound reverberates around the room and Joe jumps.

'Damn-it!' The razor nicks his throat. 'You bloody frogs have to go. You'll just have to find somewhere else to live.' Joe opens the vanity drawer. It's pointless removing the frog. It'll be back before the day is out. He scrabbles for cotton wool before realising he's in the guest bathroom and turns instead to the toilet paper roll. It isn't fair. He needs a break, a bit of excitement in his life. The frog croaks again. This time he ignores it.

An old song plays on the radio and he turns it up, singing along... 'All I want to do is make love to you.' Nostalgia for his youth swamps him, the squandered years of carefree existence, the wine bars and pubs, dim lights and music. Youth is wasted on the young, they never know what they have until it's gone. Kids don't deserve the freedom of youth. They haven't earned it. They haven't sacrificed their lives to years of grinding duty like he has.

He searches the dark irises of his eyes as he holds a wad of paper to the cut. He wants to feel his blood surging, not leaking out into toilet paper. He wants to fill the void before he dies. When he met Maggie, life was exciting, but it was a long time ago, before the séances, superstitions and alternative therapy gate crashed their lives.

Maggie's dad is probably right. Stan said the trouble with Maggie is that she doesn't have enough to fill her time now the twins are away at University. She should find a new purpose instead of frittering her days away with that mush for brains, man eating crowd of women she calls friends—wombats he called them and the name stuck in Joe's brain.

Trouble is she doesn't want for anything. It's not like they need the money and Maggie says she's not trained for anything, but dancing. If she got a full-time job it would be unfulfilling and menial, and she's happy teaching dance classes one day a week.

Unfulfilling, huh, she doesn't know the meaning of the word. Try working your butt off for twenty years, only to have some arse-creep, ten years younger, steal your promotion.

Joe washes his razor in warm water remembering his colleague Basil Lombardy, the herpetologist, who he took to identify the frogs he found at the waterfall, repeating his favourite hominy; *it's all about how much one publishes mate*. Blah, blah, blah!

Joe knows he hasn't published much over the last few years. Who has time to publish a book, teach and carry out new research with a depressed and neurotic wife to worry about at home? His life yawns before him; a dreary march along a corridor of stifling nothingness, 'and then we die,' he hears his son chant.

The trouble was his parent's insistence on him doing science at Uni. If he had rebelled then, but he never really rebelled against anything in his life, just went along with it for the sake of keeping the peace. His mother was on his side, but his dad was adamant.

'Music is his life Max,' his mother said, but his dad folded his arms and said, 'No Beth, first he gets an education. After that he can do what he wants.' There was no arguing with his father who was morose, moody or absent most of the time. His mum said it was from the Vietnam War, but for as long as Joe could remember he had tiptoed around an erratic father who was a complete stranger to him. He vowed never to do that to his own children.

Joe puts his shaving stuff back in the bag. He's left his comb in the en-suite, so he runs his hands through his hair, worrying about the increasing grey. Max had gone grey early and it looks like he's inherited the genes. Maggie calls it salt and pepper. It's just grey in Joe's book, and too long. It needs cutting. He dabbles at the razor cut, then picks up the transistor and ambles naked down the hallway to return it to the desk in the living room.

When he gets back to the bedroom, Maggie is still in the bathroom. What the hell does she do in there? He pulls on a pair of denim jeans and tee-shirt and picks up the phone extension to dial Maggie's parent's to deliver the bad news.

Her mother answers and Joe says, 'hello Elaine, it's Joe.'

'Hello dear, all set for the trip?'

'Um... Elaine... Um. We have to cancel...'

Why? What's the problem?

He pauses and then says, 'ah nothing really, except Maggie's not feeling well. We'll have to take a raincheck. I'll collect the twins.'

Joe hears the scrunching of car tyres on the gravel driveway, and walks along the corridor to look out through the laundry window, the phone still held to his ear.

There's a note of alarm in Elaine's voice. 'What's wrong with her?'

Distracted by Julian's arrival, Joe says, 'not really sure, but she'll be fine with a bit of rest. I'll just drive down and pick up the twins from Uni and come straight home.'

Outside, Julian Boradin the III pulls up on the gravelled parking area near the laundry.

Joe watches him from the window as Maggie's mum lectures him about lying.

'I can always tell when you're fibbing Joe. You shouldn't cover for her. She has to face up to her responsibilities. Now—the truth please.'

'Oh all right. She's not really sick.' He pauses.

'I'm waiting.'

'Ahh... Um... I know I shouldn't cover for her.'

Julian gets out the car and looks around, swivelling on his heel as if surveying his own estate.

'Sorry Elaine, I missed that?'

'What is the real problem?'

'Um... Oh, well... Um... It's a premonition apparently.'

Julian shuts the car door.

'A premonition!' Elaine moderates her tone and asks, 'what about?'

'I don't know, except she doesn't think it will be healthy to get out of bed.'

Elaine sighs. 'Her Grandmother was the same. Is she still taking the pills the doctor prescribed?'

'No, she stopped months back—said they were making her sick.'

Joe's eyebrows climb as he watches Julian take out an expensive designer labelled carryall from the boot of his car. 'What student has that much money?'

'Pardon?'

'Oh, sorry Elaine I wasn't talking to you.'

'Look Joe. I think we should come up. This isn't right. I tell

40

you what, we can pick up Paul and Abigail and bring them home. It'll save you the trip. We'll spend a few days at the farm just to make sure she's all right. I want to see my grandchildren, and Stan will be disappointed to hear you aren't coming. He can collect them from Uni now, and we can drive up to the farm tomorrow afternoon. Stan will want to show off the new boat, so he can take them for a spin later today or tomorrow morning before we leave.'

'Ah, you don't need to do that...'

Julian places a shiny new Akubra on his carefully combed blond hair. Wanker, Joe thinks turning his back to the window, to focus on what Elaine is saying.

'It'll be fine, besides I want to see how my daughter is doing.'

Relief floods through Joe. Perhaps Elaine will shed light on Maggie's weird behaviour. 'Well if you're sure—that's good of you. You're sure Stan won't mind.'

'He'll mind, but he'll get over it.'

'Okay. The kids will be happy if they get to see the whales.' Joe turns back to look out the window again, but Julian has disappeared. Where did he go?

'There are no guarantees they'll see any whales. The season is just about finished.'

'No you're right. Are you sure you don't need me to come down?'

'It'll be fine dear. You'll phone the twins to let them know Pops is coming?'

'Yes. I'll do that now. We'll see you tomorrow then— evening-ish.'

'I look forward to it.'

Elaine says the last bit dryly and Joe winces, but is relieved. He flicks through the phone for Paul's number.

Paul groans as Joe explains the change in plans, but makes no other comment. Joe asks him to pass on the message to his sister.

As he hangs up, he feels like a coward. He knows he should phone Abby himself, but he can't face it, can't deal with the interrogation and accusations.

He walks across the room to open the laundry door for Julian. They'll have a full house over the next few days, and unless he tells Julian to go away, Maggie will need to get another room ready for her parents.

Joe likes Maggie's parents, but Stan will be furious. He's missing the best fishing weather, and will make sure his son-in-law pays. Joe sighs again. If only he didn't feel so responsible for everyone else's behaviour and happiness.

How's he going to tell Julian to go away? The bloke said on the phone last night he was looking forward to having a rest in the country after the grind of finishing his dissertation. Joe hasn't the heart to say he can't stay. What does an extra person matter? They have plenty of room although he doesn't like Julian much. Last time he and his friend Anton came up here, they made Joe feel uncomfortable. There is something predatory about the blokes.

Maggie feigned shock, saying it was prejudice because they're gay. Joe is still dubious about that. He saw Anton's relentless pursuit of Trish at the club. The man didn't look gay to him. Julian, on the other hand, is a different matter. Joe sneers as he remembers the bloke's poncy designer labels and his finickiest about his hair.

He looks out the laundry door. Where the hell has the bloke gone?

Maggie walks past him down the hallway, buttoning up a filmy white blouse. She wears cut-off pants and her feet are bare. 'Why the big sigh? No Joe, don't open that door. I'll get the front door. You can't have guests coming through the laundry. Really!'

'I thought it was too dangerous to get out of bed today.'

'Tch.' His derision annoys her. 'It's going away that's

dangerous not staying at home. If I stay here everything will be fine. I told you what my horoscope said.'

'I thought it was a dream.'

'Oh Joe, for goodness sake. The dream was a premonition that something bad would happen, but my stars say I need to be a homebody this week, and everything will work out fine. Clearly, it means going away equals bad, staying home equals good. See, that's not too hard to understand, is it?'

He bites back his retort and says instead, 'oh great, does that mean you are going to cook breakfast then? I would kill for bacon and eggs.'

'No. It's oats and yogurt.'

'Why can't we have bacon and eggs? I'm on holiday.'

'I don't think there's enough defrosted, and you shouldn't eat bacon. It's full of nitrates; do you want to make my premonition come true by having a heart attack, like your father?'

Joe opens his mouth to respond, but the front door bell interrupts.

'I'll just let Julian in?' Maggie skips down the corridor.

Joe calls after her. 'What will you tell him? Are you going to say you had a premonition?'

'Yes.'

'No, seriously?'

Maggie stops. 'Yes. Anyway, we can't send him away. He gave up the lease on his flat because he's only got a week before he goes home to New York. I said he and Anton could stay until they go.'

'Looks like Anton's not coming.'

'He might come later. Julian was a bit vague.'

Maggie opens the door into the entrance hall and glances in the mirror. She straightens her blouse and smooths her hair.

As Joe turns towards the kitchen, he hears her voice drift

along the corridor. 'Hello Julian. Come in. Congratulations on completing your PhD. Here put your bag down and come into the kitchen. I'm just going to make breakfast.'

A deeper voice murmurs and Maggie giggles.

It sets Joe's teeth on edge. She's too old to giggle like that. It was cute when he first met her, but now it sounds ridiculous. She claims its nerves, and she can't help it, but it's embarrassing. All he asks is that she controls it in public. Surely she can manage that.

He strains to hear what they're saying, but he can only hear fragments of their conversation until Maggie exclaims, 'oh are you? Well, bacon and eggs coming right up.'

Joe's throat tightens as the door's crystals tinkle on the closing breeze. He stomps into the kitchen to make coffee. As he grinds the beans, Julian walks in behind him.

'Hello sir.'

Joe ignores him, pretending the coffee grinder has drowned out his voice.

Maggie follows. 'Joe, Julian said hello.'

Joe turns. 'Oh yes, I see. I suppose you want coffee too?'

'Oh Joe, not coffee. Have herbal tea. Coffee is poison, you know that. You're too old to abuse your body like this.'

Joe grits his teeth. How can she say such things and think that it's okay? But it's not Julian's fault. He can't have an all-out domestic spat in front of the student. He adopts a friendlier tone. 'I suppose Maggie told you we're not going?'

'Yes.' Julian looks embarrassed. 'She's had a premonition or something.'

'That, and her horoscope,' Joe says dryly.

'Pardon?'

'Nothing.'

When the coffee perks, Joe pours himself a cup and tells

Julian to help himself. Then he takes his coffee out to the garden. He is outraged at Maggie offering to cook Julian bacon and eggs while she makes him eat oats. Not that he doesn't like it, he does. In fact he enjoys a good bowl of porridge. It's the principle. He doesn't want to make a scene. At least, she could also make oats for Julian, but darling Julian doesn't eat oats, says it's for horses. What is he then, a horse? What is the purpose of keeping chickens if they don't eat their bloody eggs?

Joe breathes in the clean morning air, and feels the resentment towards his wife, dissipate. He sits on a bench under the rose arbour he built for her when they first arrived at the farm. Beneath his feet, oregano covers the ground under the table and creeps across to climb over a rock wall nearby. His boots bruise the leaves and they fill the air with scent.

He can't bear being indoors all day, especially with Julian there. Perhaps he'll take a trek through the forest to the waterfall and check on the frogs. He'll take a packed lunch and spend the day collecting photos and information for his book.

The fresh breeze, along with the morning aromas of coffee, bacon frying, dew-drenched lawn, damp forest, rose-blossoms, and oregano, lift his spirits. Contentment seeps through his shoulders as he sips his coffee, and gazes across the landscape to the distant mountains.

Long tubes of dense white cloud weave through valleys, leaving sunlit hilltops hovering above the mist. A new harmonic forms in his mind. The forested mountains, the mist, and rain-green paddocks, give a lift to his mood as the imagined music swells. Mentally, he scratches out the music so he won't forget. He incorporates grace notes to reflect the lingering squawks, whistles and burbles of the dawn chorus while he stares out at cattle ruminating in the field.

A memory intrudes, interrupting the music, and he worries

about the calves. Just a few days ago Callum, a neighbouring farmer, uncovered a dingo den when clearing weeds in a gully on his farm. Five dingos escaped, crossing into the National Park. Now he wonders if he should consider poison baits. He'll have to do it secretly because Maggie won't hear of it.

Julian interrupts Joe's contemplation. 'Breakfast is ready Dr. Williams,' he says coming around the side of the house from the terrace.

Joe waits until he's gone back inside before following him. They are sitting at the kitchen table when he walks in. Maggie has a pot of yogurt in front of her. Julian has a plate of bacon and eggs. At the end of the table, closest to the door, a steaming bowl of porridge waits for him. Joe feels his jaw clench. He picks up the bowl and walks out without a word.

Maggie stares after him, annoyed by her husband's rudeness to their guest, even if it's just Julian. It's still boorish, and anyway she already told him there wasn't enough defrosted bacon. Julian won't eat oats. Joe knows that, and he likes porridge. The man is full of contradictions this morning. If he wanted eggs, he should have gone to see if the hens have laid any. He could also defrost bacon from the freezer. She doesn't understand him lately. He knows she has run down the perishables in the fridge because they were to go away this morning.

Joe pauses at the doorway. He realises his behaviour is offensive and feels an attack of guilt at his ungraciousness. Julian, is a guest. 'I'll be in the sitting room, watching the news,' he says giving him a small nod as he walks out.

The morning news report includes the usual mayhem of traffic accidents, politics and a piece about a local prison break. 'Huh,' Joe slurps porridge into his mouth, 'only in North Queensland would anyone think a hundred plus kays, is local.' Lucky Maggie isn't watching.

Joe turns off the television and walks back to the kitchen with his empty bowl. As he passes the piano, he runs his fingers across the panelling. He rarely finds time for it anymore although Maggie badgers him to play when she dances. The last time he did, Julian waltzed her around the floor. The ponce looked professional. Another black mark as far as Joe is concerned, but he'll have to practice if he's to accompany Lexi.

When he gets to the kitchen he looks out the window and sees Maggie and Julian walking towards the chook pen. Julian carries the hen's grain. Joe pinches the scraps of left over bacon from the pan and stuffs them into his mouth, closing his eyes with pleasure at the saltiness. Then he sets about making sandwiches to take with him on his trek to the waterfall. There is nothing worthwhile in the fridge. He can't be bothered going to the veggie garden for salad stuff and settles for tinned corned beef and cheese.

The outside door slams as Maggie re-enters the house, humming a tune. He calls out, 'how many eggs did they lay this morning?' There's a muffled response he doesn't catch, but it doesn't matter. He's not interested. 'Oh, and Mags, I think I might head over to the waterfall for a few hours, check on the frogs, see if any survived and get photos for my book, okay.'

Maggie walks into the kitchen, pushing stray strands of hair behind her ears. 'Sorry, what did you say? …Oh Joe not corned beef and cheese. You know how bad it is.'

'There's nothing in the fridge for sandwiches for my trip. Perhaps you might find the time to go shopping today if you think your grandmother's ghost will let you.'

Maggie feels a sharp surge of anger, but she doesn't want another argument and walks out the kitchen. Bugger him; let him have a holiday with the kids. She'll manage happily without his sarcasm for a day or two.

Joe packs his sandwiches into the backpack along with a water bottle, and puts the satellite navigator, and Swiss army knife, the twins gave him last Christmas, into his pocket.

6.

Vainglory

'God, they're so selfish.' Abby is in her room at the university hall of residence. She sits on a suitcase trying to lock it as Paul delivers Joe's message. Her hair is blonde like her mother's, but hangs in waves down her back.

'Now instead of four hours till they get here, I only have an hour before Pops arrives. It's not enough time. I wanted to go shopping.' The suitcase pinches her. 'Ow, that hurt.' She sucks the edge of her hand and looks up at her brother. 'Why aren't they coming, what's happened?'

Paul gazes at her with level grey eyes and ignores her question. 'Do you want a hand with that?'

'Duh—obviously,' she says abandoning her attempt to close the bloated case.

'Crikey Abbs, how do you collect so much stuff?'

She ignores him. 'Why aren't they coming?' She scrutinises her brother's face. 'You're not telling me everything.'

Paul mumbles as he kneels beside her to shut the suitcase.

'What? You're mumbling again. You're covering up something.'

'It's nothing.' Paul runs his fingers over his lips. Dark stubble covers his cheeks, and hair the same colour, flops down into his eyes.

'Liar, I can tell by your mouth you're lying. Ha! You can't hide it. You and Dad do the same thing.' She punches his arm. 'Stop ignoring me... It's something weird isn't it? That's why you won't tell me. Why didn't Dad ring me? He never rings me. He only ever rings you when there's bad news.' Paul's lips set in a white rimmed line so she tries wheedling. 'Tell me, pleeease.'

He sits back on his haunches sighing, and rubs his arm. 'It's nothing Abbs, let it go. Pops and Gram have offered to pick us up that's all. We'll stay at their place tonight, go out in the boat with Pops, and they'll take us home tomorrow arvo. Dad says Gram and Pops will spend a few days at our place. That's it, nothing else.'

'Liar, Mum's had a breakdown again, hasn't she?'

'No she hasn't. Seriously, she's fine.'

'I'm going to ring her. Oh—give me your phone. I've got no credit.'

'No.'

Abby pushes Paul onto her suitcase as she tries to get his phone from his pocket. Paul stands up with her hanging onto his back. He twists out from her grasp, and grabs her wrists. 'Stop or I'll Chinese burn you.'

'Oh all right, but please tell me.' Abby gazes at her twin tearfully. 'You never tell me anything.'

'That's because you're flaky and can't keep secrets.' Paul lets go of Abby's wrists.

'Can. Please Paul, I promise.'

'Oh all right, but don't get all hissy-fit on me.'

'Promise.' Abby crosses her heart.

'Mum dreamed a premonition, a warning or something...'

'I knew it. It's terrible. What will happen to me? Mum always knew it would be something horrible. That's why she's so scared when we are away.'

'Gees, Abby, not you. Mum.'

'Oh... Is she going to die or something?' Abby's eyes cloud.

'Don't be stupid. That's why I didn't tell you. You always imagine the worst or think it's about you. Dad didn't know anyway, just said she couldn't travel so the hols at Gram and Pops is off. They're coming to ours instead. It's not serious, okay.'

'God, they are so selfish.' Abby says again and throws herself down on her bed. 'They're ruining my life. Why couldn't Dad come and get us. It's his fault isn't it? Mum wouldn't be so bloody superstitious if he paid her some attention. He's such a chauvinist, always thinks he knows what's best for everyone. If he paid Mum half the attention he pays those bloody frogs, she wouldn't be like this... Bugger... If I can't go shopping, Gram will have a fit. I've done no washing and have no clean clothes to wear.'

Paul turns back to the case, ignoring her as he re-folds her clothing.

Abby lolls on the bed while her twin repacks. 'I will never get married, ever. I'm never going to let a man ruin my career like Dad did to Mum.'

'Bullshit.'

'It's true. Mum would have been a famous ballerina if Dad hadn't come along and got her pregnant with us.'

'Rubbish, who told you that crap?'

'I overheard Gram and Pops talking about it.'

'That's just junk. Dad was the one who sacrificed his career. If we hadn't come along he'd be famous now, like that bloke Rachmaninoff.'

'Who?'

'I don't know; a Russian composer bloke who played the piano. Dad's hero anyway.'

'How do you know that?' Abby watches Paul with furrowed brow, her long elegant fingers plucking at the neck of her tee-shirt.

'He told me.'

Abby's eyes fill with tears.

'How come he told you that, and he didn't tell me?'

'Ah Abbs, he doesn't cut you out you know. You're a bit scary to tell things to, and you ask so many bloody questions.'

'Well how come he told you then and...'

'He told me because I didn't know what I wanted to study at uni, had no idea. You are so organized and certain about your goals. You always knew you wanted to be an artist, but I hadn't a clue. Dad told me to follow my dreams, not think about a career, not think about making money and just do what I love. He told me about his dream of becoming a concert pianist. First, his dad made him study science at Uni. Said he had to get a proper education. Then he met Mum when he was playing in a bar while he finished his PhD, and she came in with her friends. Anyway, when we came along, he had to give it up to help Mum and took on a job as tutor. He said he probably wouldn't have made it anyway, said everyone has dreams about fame and fortune when they're young, but he would never know.'

'That's so sad... but Dad's got money, why did he need to work.'

'Because, he didn't then. It was before Granddad died and left that money. Before anyone knew he was rich.'

'Who cares? The only thing I want to know is why we can't touch the Trust until we are twenty-one. I need the money now, not when I'm ancient. Grandad Max was weird. Dad never talks about him, and there are no photos anywhere. Remember that sympathy card he left Mum and us in the will?'

'Dad said that was just his warped sense of humour, like he was commiserating with Mum for having married Dad.'

Abby gets off the bed and bends to hug Paul as he kneels on the floor. 'Poor Dad... Phew, you stink. You've still got on the same clothes you wore to the party last night.'

Paul pushes the case closed and clicks the catch shut. 'So, what's it to you?'

'You slept with someone, didn't you? I can tell. You reek of it.' She examines his reddening face. 'Ha! It was one of those German backpackers—the blonde one—you were all over her last night. Um-ah, she's much older than you.'

'No, she's not. She's only twenty two.'

'I bet she bribed you.'

'No she didn't—why would she?'

'You told her where the waterfall is, didn't you? She was going on about photographing that frog that Dad discovered, and you gave in and told her. Ha, ha, you're in trouble.' Abby sings the last phrase.

'No one will know.' Colour rises up Paul's neck. 'I made her promise not to tell anyone, and to be careful.'

'Dad will be wild.'

'You're not going to tell him!'

'Hm, we'll see about that.' She flings her hair behind her shoulders and leans out the window. 'Jess, Jessica, wait up.' She turns to Paul. 'What time is Pops coming?'

'At ten. He said for us to be waiting in the car park, but Abb...'

'Okay, see ya...' Abby races out the room leaving Paul holding her suitcase.

An hour later, Stan sits behind the steering wheel of his four by four. He's parked with the motor running and the air-conditioner on, waiting for his granddaughter. She's late. She is always late. He thrums his fingers on the steering wheel.

Paul hunches in the passenger seat, wishing his sister would be on time, just once in her life. At that moment Abby comes into view, dawdling across the Campus car park with her friend Jessica. Pops gives no sign he's seen her and stares ahead, but Paul knows he's impatient by his drumming fingers. It's Stan's one give-away.

He remembers when Pops taught him to play poker. 'The thing is, no one can truly hide their emotions if you know what to look for,' he told Paul. 'All you need to watch for is the minute expansion of a pupil, the infinitesimal flicker of an eyelid, or maybe the twitch at the corner of a mouth— remember, the slightest wrinkle of a nostril, movement of a brow, or a flick of your opponents gaze will tell you all you need to know.'

Pops is pretty good, but he forgets his hands. Paul smiles; it's not a mistake he makes.

Gram told him off for teaching Paul to play poker. 'You are teaching the child vice.'

Pops said, 'but he's winning. The boy's a natural.'

Gram gave one of her stern looks, and Stan said, 'it's only matches Elaine.'

Gram won. Gram always wins, and Pops put the matchsticks away. Paul was disappointed. Pops is good to get alone when Gram is not listening. The stories he tells about his years as a police officer are exciting.

Boys-own adventures, Dad calls them, and warned Paul not to believe everything Stan tells him.

Paul once thought he might become a police officer, but Pops said, 'it's not the same anymore son. Nowadays all they do is sit behind computers scratching their arses. It's not the policing I remember when we were out and about catching crooks, not filling in paperwork.'

Paul watches Abby as she walks across the car park with Jess. A group of students stop chatting to watch the girls pass. Why is it that pretty girls always walk as if the world is watching them? Perhaps because they know it is. That's what Paul likes about Tatjana, the German woman he met last night. She doesn't need an audience.

Abby and Jess reach the car. They kiss goodbye. That also puzzles Paul. Why does his sister have to kiss and touch everyone? Paul once thought Jess hot stuff. He had a crush on her before he met Tatjana. Now, the beautiful German backpacker is the love of his life.

Abby saunters over to the driver's window and kisses Pops on his rasping cheek. 'Hi Pops…'

'Where's your port Abigail?' He says, looking for her suitcase.

'Paul was supposed to bring it.' She glares at her twin.

'Go and get it Paul.'

'But Pops…'

'Just get it, there's a good man. If we let Abigail go, we could wait here all day.'

Paul scowls at Abby as he gets out the car. 'Slag,' he hisses so Pops can't hear. He knows she will take the front seat, but there's nothing he can do, not in front of Pops anyway. He will get pay-back later.

'So childish,' she retaliates, poking her tongue at him as she climbs into the front seat where she subsides with hands folded in her lap. While they wait, she answers her grandfather's questions about her studies, and her friends, until she sees Paul walking back across the car park, carrying her heavy suitcase.

'Right, in the back girlie,' Stan orders as Paul puts her case in the boot.

'Aw, Pops…'

'Don't argue with me young lady, you're not too big to put over my knee. Now do as you're told and get in the back seat so I can plan the boat trip with your brother.'

Paul opens the car door for Abby to get out. He runs his fingers over his lips, barely hiding his triumph at her scowling face.

'You'll pay,' she hisses as she pushes past him. 'I'll tell Dad about Tatjana and the waterfall.'

Paul blanches, but it's too late to say anything, so he brings out his reserve and mouths, 'ecstasy,' at her, but she isn't looking.

There are a few things about his sister's activities he's sure she wouldn't want Pops to hear. Activities like the ecstasy she took with Jess a few weeks ago. Paul had to use his pitiful allowance to get her back to campus in a taxi because she told strangers in the street she loved them. She owes him. Pops would do his nut if he found out about the drugs. He was rabid when it came to that sort of thing, going off, red faced about having spent his whole working life fighting crime so that his grandchildren wouldn't be exposed to the stuff.

Pops looks at his watch. 'We'll just make the next ferry. You know what your Gram's like about punctuality.'

7.

Temptation

Julian stands in the vegetable garden holding a basket while Maggie cuts a lettuce for lunch. He adjusts the front of his white linen shirt as his scrutiny travels along the faint outline of her breasts, showing through the filmy material of her blouse, and travels around her curved posterior, down her legs, admiring the muscled thighs, round calves and neat ankles. She is a fine piece of ass. A worthy conquest before he departs these shores, forever.

She has the legs of a dancer, and oh how she can dance. He remembers the conference where they met. Joe gave a keynote address and went to bed early with a headache. Julian and Anton, along with some of Joe's students, took Maggie and her friend Trish out dancing. What a night.

Julian decides he will have Maggie before he leaves. He failed last time, surprised at her resistance. Never before had a woman thwarted his advances to the extent Maggie did. She has become a special challenge. He counts himself lucky she isn't going away for the weekend after all. It means he has one last shot at seduction. He won't blow it this time.

That husband of hers is such a looser. Julian can't see what Maggie sees in him. Typical mediocre boffin in a backwaters' university—Julian can't stand academics and hated having to come to Australia to finish his studies, but it was that or having to endure the humiliation of his parents' control. It's all that tattletale bitch-friend of his mother's fault.

'What will you do now you've finished your dissertation Julian?' Maggie stands. A pile of salad vegetables sits on the ground next to her. She stretches her back before bending to gather them up to put in the basket. He smells of pine scented cologne, and she wrinkles her nose in mild aversion to its sharpness.

His gaze lingers on her lips. 'I will spend every minute of every day in adoration of you, lovely Maggie.'

'Silly.' She laughs and drops her knife into the basket. 'Come along. Let's check if those naughty girls have laid any more eggs.' She closes the gate to the garden. 'Seriously Julian, what are your plans? You'll leave for America next week and then what? Will you join your father's business or do something else, teach perhaps? What does a Rainforest Eco specialist, do other than teach?'

Julian's eyelids droop as his lips tighten. He doesn't want to think about going home, not now. 'Yeah,' he mumbles, 'family business summons—imperiously. Can we talk about something else?' He clears his throat and tries another line, putting his hand on her hip. 'You're gorgeous, you know that.'

It comes out wrong, and she reacts. 'Stop it Julian. I'm old enough to be your mother.'

'Not quite, you haven't seen my mother.'

Julian lapses into silence as they walk to the hen house, his long legs striding ahead, putting distance between them. He doesn't want the conversation about his parents and going home to continue. There are eight days left of freedom, and he's determined to make the most of it.

Maggie regrets snapping and calls after him. 'When we've finished with the hens Julian, I'll do my exercises. Will you dance with me? You are such a beautiful dancer, and it's more fun having someone to do it with, rather than practicing by myself.' She catches up with him. 'Wait up; I can't keep up with you. We'll move the chairs to make room like we did when Anton and Trish were here. That was so much fun, do you remember on the Queen's Birthday weekend?'

He hands her the basket and ducks into the hen house. She

waits by the door. 'You and Trish were rock and rolling and you collided with Joe, nearly knocking him off the piano stool.' Maggie giggles at the memory.

How could he forget, especially Joe's controlled fury, saying, 'I think that's enough?'

Julian places his expensive trainers carefully as he searches the boxes for eggs.

'You're such a brilliant dancer.' Maggie waits, but there's no reply. 'Can you hear me in there?'

He comes out holding six eggs, which he lays in the basket of vegetables. 'Yes I hear you. I'm afraid years of expensive ballroom dancing classes have given me that dubious honour. Will Dr. Williams play?'

'No, he's gone to Townsville to collect the twins. It's just you and me.'

'Oh, I didn't hear him go.' Julian looks towards the house as a thrill of anticipation shoots through him, crowding out thoughts of his mother. He will have Maggie all to himself.

Maggie chews her lip and frowns. 'He's cross with me for mucking things up. Now he's gone off in a huff.' She glances up at Julian, her brow clearing. 'I read his stars so I am not worried about him. He will be all right. His are excellent, it's only mine that say I must stay at home.'

They walk to the terrace, and Julian goes ahead into the sitting room, stopping to gaze at his reflection in the grey glass of the sliding doors, pursing his lips at the image. His hands smooth combed hair, and dust an imagined spec off his shoulder. 'What about my stars then?'

Maggie walks up behind him. 'You're a Leo like Joe, aren't you, just a different decan? Your stars are perfect. You have Venus moving through your sign. It's retrograde, but that's not all bad. You will still feel the spell of love, but will likely see an unexpected turn of events.'

At that moment, Joe pokes his head around the sitting room door from the hallway. 'Well I'll be off then. I've made sandwiches, and I have the sat nav and camera, in case you are looking for either of them. I might be late getting back, but don't worry I'll be fine. Behave yourselves.'

Julian marshals a bland expression. 'Have a good trip Dr. Williams.'

Joe responds, 'perhaps if you are doing nothing, you can water the cattle and give them molasses.' He's gleeful at Julian's glum expression. It will serve the little poof right—the bacon stealing thief.

Maggie crosses the room. 'Joe, I thought you'd left already.' She kisses him on the cheek. 'Come home safely.'

While Maggie goes to put the produce away in the kitchen, Joe disappears down the hallway towards the connecting door to the garage. Julian remains in the sitting room gazing at his reflection until Maggie returns and selects a CD from the bookshelf.

'A quick-step I think, to get the blood racing,' she says as she turns up the volume.

The staccato sound of a saxophone fills the room, introducing Elvis Presley's *Witchcraft*. Julian turns from his reflection in the glass doors to take Joe's wife into his arms. Maggie leans back looking into his broad tanned face as they step around the sitting-room floor and out through the sliding doors to the terrace.

'Julian, am I as old as your mother?'

'Christ no! She's a hundred.'

Maggie laughs. 'Nonsense, I bet she is gorgeous. Rich American women always are, aren't they?'

'Maggie. Please don't compare yourself with my mother. You are beautiful. But you know that already.'

'Do you like older women? You seemed to like Trish a lot.'

'Don't tease Maggie. It's only you I fancy. Why do you think I'm here?'

Maggie tilts her head and looks at him from under lowered lashes. 'Joe thinks you're gay you know.'

'Does he?' Julian's mouth purses. 'Why does he think that then?'

'I told him you were ages ago, when you first brought Anton up here.'

'You're a bad girl.'

'I also told him you were bringing Anton with you to stay this holiday.'

'Oh—he didn't ask where Anton is.'

'No. He thinks he's coming later. It's so much easier when husbands think men are gay. There's no pawing at the ground, or beating the chest all the time.'

Julian ignores the mixed metaphor. 'I wondered why he left you alone with me. He doesn't think I'm any threat.'

Maggie laughs. 'No, and you aren't you know.'

'Aren't what?'

'You aren't a threat.'

Julian groans. 'Maggie please, I am your slave. I'm dying for you.'

'Hm... Just the way it should be.'

He pulls her to him, crushing her against his muscled chest. She breathes him in before pushing him away.

'Really Julian, I am a married woman.'

'You're a terrible tease, that's what you are.'

'And,' she stops dancing to tuck stray strands of hair behind her ears, 'as I told you before, you are young enough to be my son.'

He puts his hand below her chin, lifting it to look into her eyes. The blood surges into her face. She casts her eyelashes down as he leans forward to kiss her.

Maggie pushes him away. 'No Julian.'

'Yes, Maggie.'

Flirting has gone from happy chatter to something too dangerous. How does Trish get away with it? She turns away and walks toward the hallway door.

'I'll make us a cup of tea, and we should give the cows molasses. I'll get something from the freezer for dinner. We can have salad for lunch. Do you like to take a nap after lunch when you're on holidays Julian? Or read a book? I like to read. I'll see if the hens have laid any eggs. There should be at least three or four more. The lazy girls.' Maggie clamps her jaw. Nervousness makes her gabble.

Power surges through Julian as he watches, amused by her loss of confidence. All things are possible after all. It just takes planning, and a cancellation of his current plans to drive into the village to see Trish tonight. Sometimes, he's amazed by his luck.

Maggie walks past the kitchen and out to the garden, her mind a kaleidoscope of anxiety. She stares at the roses. They fall in profusion, rampant, red, and luxuriant, shading the garden table from the summer heat. She's out of her depth, and she knows it.

Suddenly, she wishes Joe was here. Why didn't she ring Julian and tell him not to come? It's all very well wanting excitement, but she's playing with fire and doesn't want to get burned.

Anxiety gnaws in her stomach as she remembers her premonition. Is this what the warning meant? Not Julian. No, she's sure it's the same as before, like the one all those years ago in Sydney, or she wouldn't feel so scared.

Joe mocks her beliefs, but he doesn't know. She has told no one about the last time, not all of it anyway. When the police asked for a description, she said she didn't get a good look at any of them. She can't tell, in case the robber keeps his threat to hurt the twins. She won't risk it. The premonition last night wasn't specific, but she knows something will happen today, something bad, like the last time.

She should have rung Trish to find out what it meant, but her horoscope said she should stay at home this week. So it can't be anything to do with her home. It isn't Joe or the kids. Why can't she shake the feeling?

She won't go shopping either, just in case he's around and recognises her. Then he'll know where to find the twins. He will never recognise them, they were too small, and he never saw Joe so it's only her that needs to stay hidden.

That he is searching, she is certain. Joe calls it superstitious mumbo jumbo, but Maggie knows she's psychic. Her grandmother told her many times—'you were born with the Caul dear.'

She was right. Look at when she and her friends went into that bar and heard Joe playing the piano. She knew she would marry him. Joe laughed at that. He said it wasn't psychic, it was scheming.

Before she met Trish, she hadn't dared tell anyone the full story, and even Trish only knows about the premonition and the bank robbery, not the robber's threat or that she can still describe all of them to their last detail, including the signature on the Jackal tee-shirt one of the men was wearing. She doesn't think they were ever caught.

She wrenches off the heads of dead roses as she remembers Joe's ridicule. He thinks I'm stupid, just because I don't have a degree. I've seen him rolling his eyes when they come for a séance, but at least I have a chance of being warned next time, and I won't ignore it.

Maggie hates wilted roses. They spoil the look of the garden, making the bushes look tatty, wrinkled and brown. They remind her of her own mortality, aging and death. She walks to the garden bench and sits down with a thump of sadness.

Joe says she's depressed because she has nothing to do, but he's just a man, what does he know about the aching void in her life. A void he hasn't even tried to fill although she's devoted her life to him and the children. Maggie feels her eyes stinging with self-pity.

She knows she's pushing Joe away, but she can't help it. She lied to him this morning, about Julian and Anton, but she was angry at his smug condescending patience. He treats her like a fragile child. Something to play with when his head isn't buried in his bloody text books. He doesn't recognise she has her own mind. She isn't stupid.

He's had all the opportunities, more than she ever had. He says she's beautiful, but he doesn't see her—not really, didn't even notice her new hair style with the highlights that make her blonde hair shimmer. Julian noticed as soon as he came in the front door.

He pulled her into an embrace, inhaling her scent, and kissed her cheek. 'Vanilla cookies,' he said pretending to faint with adoration.

She giggled then, she couldn't help it. He is so, so, she struggles to find the right word—romantic, daring, young and fearless.

She and Joe have nothing in common any more. Now the children are gone, they only talk about the humdrum necessities of daily life. They no longer dream, or plan for a future. They have nothing left to strive towards. It's all behind them; memories of better days gone, with nothing but fear of discovery, by a murderous robber, as she waits at home through the long, lonely years that stretch ahead, endless and unvarying.

'Tea, for my beautiful doll-eyes.' Julian walks towards the

rose arbour carrying two mugs of tea.

'Oh Julian, I'm sorry I forgot. I was supposed to make the tea and now you've done it. Thank you.'

He places the mugs on the table and walks behind her to massage her shoulders.

'You're so tense, my love.'

Maggie relaxes. A massage won't get her into any trouble, and it feels so good. She leans back against his hard stomach, and his hands slip around her neck and down the front of her blouse.

She jerks forward. 'Julian don't...'

He grins. 'You can't blame a man. You are too, too, tempting a morsel.'

She forces a smile at his compliment and sips her tea. It has a funny taste, so she puts it back on the table. Why can't Joe say things to her like Julian does? It makes her feel wonderful, like she is a desirable woman, not someone who has passed her prime.

Julian sits next to her, the length of his thigh hot-pressed along hers. 'How is Trish?'

He stares ahead, knowing it will make Maggie jealous if he talks about Trish. They are peculiar best friends. The two women seem hell-bent on assassinating each other. While he was making tea, he rang Trish to cancel their evening together, and she had some choice descriptions about Maggie, and a bloke she's seeing on the side. Just shows how you can never judge a book by its cover. He thought Maggie wasn't up for that sort of thing; always thought she was the boring faithful type.

'I haven't seen her for a couple of days, but I'm sure she's fine.'

'She was in fine form last weekend.'

'Sorry, last weekend. Was she in Cairns?' Maggie is alert, her senses tuned to nuance as she turns to look into Julian's face, searching for details. 'She didn't say.'

'Yep, she stayed at Anton's place—quite a goer, your Trish. She certainly didn't think Anton was gay.' Julian laughs at the blush spreading across Maggie's cheeks, but he notices her shoulders relax. So, she doesn't mind Trish being at Anton's.

Maggie takes another sip of tea. Trish is a free agent. What she does is nobody's business although she isn't sure she believes Julian about Trish and Anton. Trish seemed to be more interested in Julian last time they spoke, and now she's smitten with Belinda's father.

'What kind of tea have you used?' She peers into her mug at the strange concoction.

'It's chai. I found your herbs and spiced it a little. Do you like it?'

'Ah, yes, I suppose so.' Maggie doesn't want to offend him. 'It's a bit unusual.'

Julian doesn't mention he included a large shot of vodka in the mix. 'When is Dr. Williams coming home?'

'Oh, I'm not sure. Things got a bit muddly this morning when you arrived, and I forgot to ask. He said he was taking a packed lunch and the sat nav., so maybe he's planning to go out with the kids in the boat with my dad, which means he won't get back until tomorrow.'

She smiles up at him, and he takes the smile as license. She pushes him away again and moves over so her leg no longer touches his. 'I doubt the twins would let him go all the way down there, only to bring them back again without going out in the boat. Abby would be furious if she missed seeing the migrating whales. I could try to phone him, but the mobile signal is hopeless in this part of the world. If they have gone out on the boat I won't be able to contact them anyway.'

She drains the last of her tea and stands up, feeling an unaccountable flush of happiness. 'It's okay. He'll be back, when he gets home. Now, what about those cows and their molasses, I can't forget to do that and it needs a big strong man to help.' She stumbles against him and puts her hands on his shoulders to right herself. 'Gosh, sorry, clumsy me.'

'Let's get to it then.' Julian stands up and dusts off the back of his trousers, then walks off towards the cattle yards. He knows he's onto a winner.

8.

Desire

Joe cuts across the lawn to the edge of the paddock and climbs through the barbed wire. He hears the drifting notes of Witchcraft, and that unmistakable sound of Elvis singing, 'don't do that, please stop it. Please stop it now. You know I can't take it...' He sings the song under his breath as he sets off towards the edge of the forest 250 metres away.

He'll follow the river to the waterfall at the other end of his property. It's quicker to go by car along the highway and up through the National Park, but he prefers the hike through the rainforest's rugged terrain. If he collects enough data and photos, he might even finish his book.

After plunging into the forest's cool damp interior he checks his navigation and sets off due east. Under the canopy, the leaf strewn ground is ridged with tree roots and rocky outcrops. Trees, with massive buttresses, tower above him. He inhales the damp wholesome smells of the forest, and whistles in reply to a Grey Headed Robin. Then he focuses his mind on observation, keen and attentive to every detail, identifying the sounds of birds and insects.

When he reaches the river, the birds and frogs fall silent and only the sounds of cicadas fill his head with their shrill. Other than that, there's no sign of habitation until a small splash and ripple gives away the movements of an elusive turtle or platypus.

The river gurgles and tumbles its way through mountain valleys, joining with other tributaries until they merge with the mighty Johnstone River that drops 760 metres to the coast where it meanders through coastal rainforest and farms to reach the sea.

Up here the water is sweet and cool in his hot mouth. He

scoops up handfuls to drink and then dowses his head. A flat rock protrudes from the bank, and he lies back against its warmth to gaze at the sky, thinking how much he loves the peace and remoteness of the river. A scrub hen screeches and he smiles, remembering when he first heard the noise.

He had shaken Maggie awake convinced someone was out in the forest screaming for help. She mumbled, 'it's just a bird.' Then she turned away and went back to sleep while he lay rigid and disbelieving, but she had been right. She had grown up with these sounds, and he was a city boy. What did he know?

When Maggie first demanded they move here from Sydney, it took months of argument until she brought him up for a visit, and he fell in love with the place. Life has a funny way of turning out. If his father hadn't left him that money, they could never have afforded to buy this place.

He used to think he couldn't live without the city, particularly its nightlife and clubs. Then the twins arrived, and the rest dropped away, but all he regrets is the music. He has other compensations, but he did it for her, and he's glad he did.

A splash brings Joe back to the present as he sits up to see what made the sound. It's time to get going. He picks up his backpack and plunges once more into the dense jungle, trying not to disturb the animals and insects he hopes he might come across, but it's rough terrain. He slides down muddy banks and trips over protruding roots and rocks as he scrambles through dense undergrowth along the river.

The muted sound of water roaring over the cliff, reaches him, and he looks forward to a swim in the pool at the base of the falls. His stomach growls, perhaps he'll eat a sandwich first. When he reaches the cliff edge, he gazes out over the gorge as he adjusts the weight of his backpack, tightening the straps, anticipating the climb.

The river thunders over the rocky cliff face, roaring as it smashes into the billabong. Spray rises like smoke, obscuring his view, then it clears leaving its minute droplets soaking into his clothing, and clinging to his eyelashes.

Trees jostle for light either side of the river. Ferns and native bananas sprout from every crack and crevice of the cliff face, and nestle among gleaming granite boulders, slippery with spray, that surround one side of the pool.

Above the forest canopy, the sky is a fathomless blue. Thick wait-a-while lianas snake their way to the light, or fall in straggling mounds on the forest floor. Joe looks for a well-anchored vine to hang onto as he descends the cliff, careful to avoid the spiny part below the fronds.

A flash of light catches his attention. Under the rippling olive water of the billabong, he can see a wavy red movement. It comes up for air and stands with its head tilted to one side. A woman in a red bathing costume wrings water from her hair.

He's furious. This is private property. His land and he wants it to remain that way. People caused the frogs' demise; people and their lotions and sun block. He doesn't want that kind of pollution in his billabong.

Science thought these frogs extinct. As far as he knows this is the only population left, which is why he kept its location secret. The last thing he wants is a bunch of tourists infiltrating his peace and privacy and disturbing the frogs. When he allowed the newspapers to publish his photos, no inducement would convince him to reveal the location. How had this blasted woman found her way here?

The woman calls out to someone else. Joe drops to the ground at the edge of the trees surrounding the water hole, just as another woman emerges from behind giant boulders. She walks naked across a stretch of sandy beach, watching where she places her feet.

Joe's breathing sounds loud in his ears and the skin on his neck prickles. He stands still, dithering with indecision, as his inaction lengthens. If he walks out of the undergrowth they'll think he was spying. He might embarrass them or worse, they'll think him a peeping Tom. Have they seen him? He doesn't know. He stares as seconds tick past, running his fingers over his mouth.

Voyeurism induces conflicting emotions, desire, guilt, and fear at being caught. He shakes his head. This is his land. Why should he feel embarrassed? They are the ones trespassing. Why is he nervous? He isn't a peeping Tom, they are on his land. Joe conjures indignation to cover his dilemma and propels himself forward.

The naked woman shades the glare from her eyes, and shrieks as he emerges. The other woman walks out the water to stand in front of her friend.

Joe cups his hands around his mouth and calls out. 'You are trespassing on private property.' The drenching spray whips his words away. He must swim across the lagoon. 'Damn them,' he mutters.

He scrambles across the rocky bank and wedges his backpack on a dry rock. It's waterproof and floats, but he doesn't want it disappearing down river. He sits down to take off his shoes. He'll leave his clothes on, but it's a warm day and they'll dry soon enough.

Across the other side of the pool, the costumed woman raises her hand in a wave. The naked woman walks away and disappears behind the rocks. She no longer seems worried, but returns moments later with a towel wrapped around her.

Joe feels a vague disappointment mingled with relief as he lowers himself into the water. It sucks the breath from his chest with its cold contrast to his hot body. As he swims his jeans drag and his tee-shirt floats up under his arms.

The women watch. Neither moves nor speaks. They remain fixed as if in fascination; a snapshot in time, until he reaches shallow water and stands, the water lapping at his waist.

'You know this is private property?'

'Ja, we have permission,' red costume says. The singsong intonation sounds Germanic to his ears.

Bullshit Joe thinks, but he says, 'from whom?'

'I beg your pardon.'

'Who gave you permission?'

'Ah.' Red costume turns to her companion. Towel woman says, 'from the owner.'

'I am the owner, and I don't recall giving you permission.' Joe tries to sound light-hearted, but only succeeds in sounding pompous. The two women look at each other puzzled.

'No—I am sorry, but the owner; we meet in Townsville with his sister. Paul tells us we can come here, but we must be careful of frogs, yes? No lotions and it must be a secret.'

'Oh.' It dawns on Joe that his children are the culprits behind this. He nods. 'You met the twins.'

'Pardon?'

'My son and my daughter, Paul and Abby—you know them— in Townsville?'

'Ja, yes.' Towel woman nods her head and turns to smile with relief at red costume.

Joe pauses for a moment wondering what he should do. When he sees the kids he'll have something to say to them, but he can't take it out on these two, if what they said is genuine. They look harmless enough. So long as they keep the secret, and keep pollutants out the water, they can't do much harm.

The red costumed girl is watching, a frown on her face. Girls, he thinks, they must be in their mid-twenties; hardly girls, but a bit old to be mixing with his kids who are nineteen. He wades through the water towards the women and clambers out onto the sandy shore.

He shrugs and holds out his hand. 'I'm Joe,' Paul and Abby's father. This is my property and I would be grateful if you can keep it secret. If too many people come here, the last remaining group of this species of frog will be gone. You wouldn't want that on your conscience would you?'

Towel woman steps closer and stretches to take his hand. Her towel slips, but she appears unconcerned as she hoists it back into position. 'I am Brigitte and here is Tatjana,' she says gesturing to red costume.

Tatjana steps forward smiling to shake his hand. Joe is having trouble maintaining his gaze at eye level and busies himself by wringing water from his tee-shirt.

Brigitte watches with a puzzled look on her face. 'Why do you not take off your clothes to swim?'

'I didn't want to frighten you.'

'Frighten us. Why would this frighten us?'

'Oh, I don't know. I was just being cautious.'

Brigitte speaks to Tatjana in German.

'Are you from Germany?'

'Ja... We are backpacking in Australia for four months now. We are told that we can get work here—farm work, fruit picking. Do you know about this?'

'I've heard about it yes, but I know little more. There's a backpacker's hostel in town; you could try that for a start. Tell me where you met Paul and Abby.'

'We meet them at a party. We have a good time.'

Joe's eyebrows rise, but he thinks it better not to pursue this line of questioning. He doesn't want to know what his kids get up to when he's not there. It's better not to ask.

'You want some tea?'

'Tea. You have tea?' Joe's surprised. He can't see any evidence of anything the women might own.

'At our camp,' Brigitte points to the rocks.

Joe assumes they have their things stashed behind the rocks somewhere, and looks at his watch. It's just past midday. 'I have sandwiches,' he points to his backpack.

'Good, get your sandwiches. We make tea.'

Joe turns to go back into the water to collect his backpack. Brigitte stops him, her hand on his arm.

'Take off your clothes. They are heavy and it's easier to swim without clothes.'

It sounds to Joe as if she thinks he's a little simple. She clearly misunderstood his intentions. He's done it from a sense of decency. What the hell if they don't mind he certainly doesn't. His underpants will keep him decent. He spreads his sodden jeans and shirt across a rock face to dry and wades back into the cold water.

Tatjana disappears behind the rock and returns with a plastic box, out of which she takes a sarong to spread across the sand. On it she lays out an assortment of food in plastic containers, a metal thermos, and three chipped enamel cups. She surveys her work and then walks to the rocky part of the water's edge, pulling on a string to bring up a wine cask bladder that's been chilling in the cold water. She smiles at Joe as he swims back with his backpack.

As they eat lunch, they swap stories. Tatjana explains she is keen to photograph the endangered frogs. She is doing a PhD at Berlin's Humboldt University. Her field is Natural Resource Management. The University's newspaper was where she first read about the frogs. The story made her keen to come to Australia.

Brigitte talks about her career as a nightclub singer. Both women are from Berlin although they only met when staying at the same Darwin backpacker hostel. Joe talks about his love of music and is surprised at how much they both seem to know about classical music.

He wonders at the courage of two young urban women, setting off alone to explore the vast continent of Australia, but he's glad they did, glad they are here and glad he's met them. As he talks about himself, the wine in his cup disappears. Tatjana fills it again, and he vows to pace himself, but the alcohol relaxes him.

Lunch is a weird mixture of left over tinned food; baked beans, dolmades, sour kraut, cheese and his corned beef and cheese sandwiches. Both women's faces crinkle with disgust when he says what the filling is so he eats them all and lies back in the sand. 'I'm stuffed,' he says patting his stomach.

Brigitte disappears behind the rocks, reappearing after a few minutes, her towel exchanged for a sarong, and a small canvass bag clutched in her hand. Her long dark hair ripples over her olive skinned shoulders.

Joe thinks she looks dangerous, older than Tatjana and less of the wholesome girl-next-door type, but more exciting. He runs his fingers across his lips and takes another gulp of wine. The sharp acidity of cheap wine trickling down his throat reminds him of his student days, and a sudden sense of liberation overwhelms him.

Brigitte pulls the sarong across her lap leaving her breasts exposed. Joe tenses, but she appears unconcerned. He averts his gaze to watch her scrabble in the canvass bag. She takes out a plastic tobacco bag, cigarette papers and a lighter. When the tobacco is rolled into a thin tube, she lights up and inhales deeply, holding the smoke in her lungs. A trickle leaks out her nostril before she makes her mouth into an O, and blows out a long stream. Joe recognises the smell from his university days. Christ, she's smoking Pot!

He's not a prude. He tried it twice at university; both times feeling very little sensation. In his opinion it wasn't all it was cracked up to be, so he hadn't bothered again. Besides he was never a rebel and each time he smoked the stuff he was terrified he'd be caught. It wasn't worth the anxiety. And it's still illegal. He has his position to consider. His hand runs over his mouth, pulling his bottom lip; what to do?

Tatjana takes the cigarette from Brigitte, drawing in and holding her breath as she hands it to Joe. He takes it, knowing he shouldn't, but he takes it anyway, sucking on the joint held between his thumb and index finger, and coughs. They laugh and he nods his thanks. Where's the harm? No one will see them here.

He sips more wine, then running his finger around his lips, he watches Brigitte light another, and takes it from her, thinking it's having little effect. It feels as if he's floating in freedom as he lies back in the sand. How lucky he didn't have to drive to Townsville. Perhaps he should thank Maggie. He closes his eyes and lets his mind drift.

The hand on his bare chest is light, almost a whisper of touch as it draws circles. He hardly dares open his eyes. Another hand touches his thigh. His lids fly open, and his breath shallows. Hovering above him are Brigitte's pointed breasts with their large brown areoles.

Tatjana sits cross legged gazing across the billabong as she draws spirals around his nipples. Brigitte presses her breasts against his shoulder as she takes his bottom lip between her teeth. He groans and returns the kiss, her mouth hot and wet against his. Through the marijuana induced haze, he thinks he shouldn't be doing this.

Brigitte's tongue runs around his lips before she sits astride him and turns to Tatjana. He watches, unmoving, as she twists her body to kiss Tatjana. His heart thuds as she lowers the shoulder straps of the red costume, tugging it down to reveal plump creamy breasts.

Without thought, Joe's hand reaches up to touch the rosy pink nipples. He's lost in the moment, with time standing still, every sense heightened by a sublime sense of acute tingling awareness. When Tatjana reaches for the wine and pours more into their mugs, he runs his palm across her back, feeling the softness of her skin. With her mouth full of cool wine she leans over and takes him in her mouth. Brigitte kneels at his side to roll another joint. The afternoon disappears in a soft glow of hedonism as Joe loses himself in a haze of pleasure.

Hours later, he awakes alone on the sandy bank under a star splattered sky. He sits up and looks around the empty beach. His head hurts and his body is dew-damp and cold. Someone was thoughtful enough to cover him with a sarong, and he pulls it around his shoulders. The luminous hands of his watch tell him it's three-fifteen. Christ, what has he done?

He clutches the sarong as guilt purges waves of nausea from his stomach. Maggie will be in a panic at his failure to return. She will imagine terrible things befalling him, thinking her premonition was right. She was right. What could be more terrible than what he's done? Clouds rush to obscure the stars and rain comes in a light flurry. He pulls on his still damp clothes, and his knife falls from his pocket. As he bends to pick it up, his head spins, and he waits for the moment to pass. Then he dusts sand off the knife and goes in search of the women.

They're in a two-man tent behind the rocks, and he squeezes in between them, out of the rain. There's not much else he can do. Getting home will have to wait until daylight or he will lose his way in the forest.

9.

Seduction

Maggie lies in the bath, bubbles to her shoulders, roses clinging to the tub rim, their bruised petals giving off a perfumed sacrifice. The lyrics from Elvis's Witchcraft repeat in her head, *my head is spinning, going round and round.* She feels woozy in the hot water as she thinks about dancing with Julian. He's such a gentleman, so kind and considerate.

She felt a little odd earlier, unsteady on her feet, and wonders if it could be an inner ear infection. It's not like she feels sick or in pain, just unsteady, but pleasantly so. Julian suggested a bath to relax while he cooks dinner.

Joe never does things like that for her, and certainly never cooks. He's hopeless in the kitchen, making a mess and putting things back in all the wrong places when he cleans. Maggie prefers to do it herself. She likes her kitchen tidy.

She scoops up rose petals and holds them to her cheek. Their fragrance is strong, and like cling-film, they stick to her skin. She peels them off, swishing her fingers in the water, so they swirl and float away.

Julian collected them for her bath. He's so transparent, such a cliché, but flirting with him is fun so long as there's no kissing, no touching, other than to dance. Her inner voice breaks through the haze, you shouldn't be doing this. It's not fair on Julian, and even if she doesn't plan on doing anything more than a little harmless flirting, it's still cheating on Joe. It must stop.

She pulls herself out of the bath and reaches for a towel, then tucks her hair behind her ears. It will stop. As she searches the medicine cabinet for colloidal silver to cure her ear infection she sings. 'Don't do that, please stop it. Please stop it now.'

Outside on the terrace, Julian lights a candle in a glass and places a bowl of roses on the table. The sun is on the horizon, its dying rays pointing accusing fingers of light across the Great Dividing Range to slant across the farm paddocks.

He gazes out across the lawn into the darkening distance then returns to the sitting room to adjust the light diffuser and stands back to survey his handiwork. Everything must be perfect before Maggie arrives.

Julian is always thorough in everything he does, and has faith in his prowess. He doesn't believe in chance. Since he first seduced Valerie, the glamorous socialite whom his father had just dumped, his appetite for beautiful older women has not diminished. Father never kept his women for long. Mother wouldn't tolerate it.

Julian learned well that seduction is all about power, which is the only thing worth a shit. The ultimate thrill is total control over other people. In his view, the two ways to get it are money and sex. Until he inherits his father's money, seduction is the only tool he has.

He pours chilled white wine in one of Maggie's best crystal glasses, and from his pocket, takes out a small plastic packet. It contains several pills; four white, four blue-grey. He chooses a white one, not wanting to give her the LSD. She should be gooey and submissive with love and passion, not hallucinating or worse, having a bad trip.

The chemistry student who made them said he should be careful not to overdo it, estimating about 150mg in each tablet. One tablet is more than enough, but Julian doesn't want her too stoned so he'll give her just enough to develop the requisite glow of love for mankind. He can always give her more later.

He carries the wine through to Maggie in the bathroom. If she drinks it now he'll have her in the palm of his hand in an hour, just as they are finishing the Pasta con Polo.

'Maggie, my lovely,' he taps on the en-suite door. It swings open with the pressure of his knock.

She's wrapped in a large bath towel and stares wide eyed in surprise. 'Julian you can't come in here. I'm not decent.'

A smile plays about the edge of his sculpted lips. 'I like you indecent, Maggie.' He hands her the glass of wine and runs his hand down her damp arm before withdrawing from the bathroom.

Once back in the sitting room, he takes a memory stick from his pocket and plugs it into the stereo. It plays a repeating loop of slow jazz. There won't be any need for distractions or opportunities for her to come to her senses and bolt while he changes music. He's the master of detail. The subject is irrelevant.

This morning, when he left Cairns, he was preparing to seduce Trish tonight. Not that she would have been much of a challenge, but better than nothing. Trish hadn't been please when he phoned her with the news that Joe and Maggie weren't going on holiday, and their evening would have to be cancelled.

Maggie has dressed for dinner at Julian's insistence. He said that's his family's custom, and it would be a special favour if she would consider it. Now, as she swishes towards the sitting room, she feels self-conscious. Perhaps she should go back to the room to change. This is not the way to keep Julian at bay. She turns around, but Julian walks out the sitting room and sees her in the hallway.

His eyes glitter in the half light as he takes her hand. 'You're stunning.'

'It's a bit over the top,' she says, twisting her wristwatch.

'Let me be the judge of that.' He walks around her sniffing a faint waft of vanilla. You'd think her husband would buy her a decent perfume. She looks tantalisingly vulnerable with her blonde hair framing flushed cheeks, and an indecisive smile on her lips.

He walks in close, not touching her, but close enough to inhale her scent. 'Where is your wine?'

'Oh, I left it in the bathroom.'

'Don't move. I'll get it for you.' He goes to the bathroom and picks up her glass, noting she has only drunk a little. He may have trouble getting her to drink the whole glass with her puritanical attitude to health.

On the way back, he stops in the kitchen to pour himself a glass of wine, minus the MDMA, and returns to the living room with the bottle. Then he places her hand around the glass, twining his arm through hers as he gazes into her eyes. Their height difference makes it awkward, but he raises the glass to his mouth hoping she will do the same.

She giggles and says, 'don't Julian.'

'I can't help it. I am smitten. You wouldn't refuse a drowning man's last wish would you? Where's the harm in a toast to your beauty my lovely Maggie?'

She winces at the corniness, but takes a small sip of her wine. She doesn't want to hurt his feelings. He tilts her glass, and she drinks, then splutters and steps away, disentangling her arm from his.

He leads her to the terrace where he pulls out her chair. 'I'll get dinner and be right back, don't vanish in my absence. I want to gaze into your eyes and drink in your beauty all night.'

Maggie watches him leave and steals her resolve to behave as she tucks her hair behind her ears. Get a grip girl. You must stop this. A little voice says where's the harm? It's just dinner, and she likes someone pandering to her for a change. It makes her feel good to be admired, especially by one as young and handsome as Julian.

She gazes out into the twilight. The flattery feels good, and she knows she looks special tonight. Gentle breezes carry the scents of herbs, roses and damp grass. The mellow music reminds her of the piano bar where she and Joe met. She picks up her wine and drinks. She loves Joe. Julian is a child, but he's sweet, although his style is a little corny. She notices the flowers on the table, the candle, the dimmed lighting, and takes another sip of her wine. It has a funny taste. She shouldn't have brushed her teeth before drinking it.

Julian comes back with two bowls of pasta. The aromas of chopped basil and slithers of parmesan cheese make her mouth water with anticipation. When was the last time she indulged in Pasta? What the hell, sometimes you have to go with the flow.

He fills up their wine glasses and sits down opposite her, lifting his glass, looking over its rim into her eyes. 'To a night of passion,' he breathes.

Her heartbeat trips and she blushes. Her eyes feel huge, like they are fully opened for the first time, and her breathing feels like it's too rapid. She takes another gulp of wine to gain control over her sudden arousal. This is ridiculous; she has to get a grip.

He breaks the tension. 'By the way, you have a large frog living in the toilet bowl.'

Maggie giggles with relief. 'There are always frogs in the toilets and snakes in the ceiling in this house. What do you expect living in the back of beyond?'

He eats, and she follows, but the food is salty and too difficult to swallow. Her mouth's dry. She gulps the wine. He chats about inconsequential things. Maggie's attention wonders. She feels decidedly odd. Perhaps she's coming down with something more than an ear infection.

'Julian, I should lie down. I don't feel right.'

He takes her hand and leads her into the sitting room. Dinner lies forgotten on the terrace table. He takes her in his arms and says, 'a slow tango I think. Relax Maggie, go with the flow. Don't fight it. You'll be fine.'

She lays her head on his shoulder and sways, feeling every sinew of his body, every muscle, and every heartbeat. The cool evening air wafts in through the open glass doors. It caresses her naked shoulders and cools her flushed face. His hands are warm spots on her naked back. They feel reassuring.

She feels herself smiling, grinning like a Cheshire cat, and giggles. He lifts her chin looking into her dilated pupils as their bodies move as one, to the rhythm of the music. A surge of what can only be described as rapture overwhelms her and she inhales, breathing in the musky smell of his sweat through the sharp deodorant.

She buries her grinning face in his shoulder, and he slides his arms around her waist, drawing her closer. Her skin shrieks under his touch as he strokes her shoulders and naked back. Her fingers feel the muscles rippling under his shirt, as he lowers his mouth to hers, teasing, withdrawing, and holding his lips millimetres from hers until she seeks his mouth for herself.

'Julian I love you, I love you,' she whispers.

'I love you too Maggie. You are beautiful, and you are mine.'

He leads her to the bedroom. A nagging voice shrieks caution as she traipses behind him, but is drowned in rapture. He is an experienced lover and takes his time. Power and success give him a sense of magnanimous well-being.

Her wide eyes, the irises blackened by inflated pupils, gaze up at him. She bites her lip, struggling in protest while her body quivers from pleasure. Sensation subsumes scruples, beneath the clamour of ecstasy, her skin alive and demanding under his hunting fingers.

A noise interrupts. He stops motionless, listening. It's the sound of tyres on gravel.

'Shit!' He leaps out of bed, grabbing his trousers and shirt. It's no later than eight-thirty. That's far too early for Maggie to be in bed, without Dr. Williams raising an eyebrow.

'Maggie, get dressed and go back to the terrace so it looks like we are having dinner. Maggie, Maggie!'

'I love you Julian.' Maggie rubs her head along the pillow, stretching her naked body, curling her toes in anticipation.

'Yes I know, but your husband's home.'

The reality of her situation penetrates the chemical fog of her mind and she rolls off the bed. She pulls the bedcovers straight, and stuffs her evening gown into the chest of drawers. Then she hauls a tee-shirt over her naked torso and stands on one foot to pull on shorts. She loses her balance and topples over onto the bed, laughing.

Julian panics. 'Get up, for Christ sake Maggie.' He pulls on his jeans and crumpled shirt and bolts out of the bedroom, heading for the guest bathroom where he can straighten his clothes.

Maggie walks out of the bedroom, eyes wide, her lips pulled back in a grin, as she makes her way to the terrace, tracing her mouth with her forefinger in wonderment. When she walks into the sitting room, Julian isn't there, instead a tall, dark-eyed man, gaunt and brooding, slouches against the sliding door.

The stranger looks to be in his late thirties, dressed in black denim jeans and a black shirt. His brown boots, once expensive tooled leather, are now scuffed and battered and look to Maggie like they need a good polish. His belt buckle and studs are large, silver and shiny. He holds a canvas sports bag in his left hand. His hair is scraped back from his forehead and held by gel against his scalp.

'You aren't my husband. Who are you?' Maggie walks up to him, and peers through the dim light into his eyes. 'Do I know you? Are you one of Julian's friends?'

His dark recessed eyes look into her enlarged pupils, and he's amused at the pretty little thing before him. She's bent off her trolley. He wonders where the husband is. His gaze runs down her scantily clad body, and he notices her mussed up hair, and that her tee-shirt is on inside out. She hardly looks old enough to have a husband.

'Is your husband here darlin, or someone else maybe?'

'Yesh, Julian's here somewhere.' Maggie waves her arms about her head. He was with me, but he's vanished. She giggles again and sways towards the man who catches her, holding her steady against his chest.

'Who are you?' she tries to focus. 'I drank too much wine and I have an ear infection.'

'I'm Taylor, mam.' His eyes dance with amusement.

'Taylor tha's not a proper name tha's a surname or the name of someone who makes suits. What's your proper name?'

'No mam, Taylor is my proper name.'

'I don't think we've met before. You're very polite. Julian!' Maggie calls out, 'your friend Taylor is here and he's very polite.'

Julian comes into the sitting room with another man walking behind him.

'Oh there you are. Where's my husband, you said he was here?' Maggie points to the man behind Julian, 'tha's not my husband.'

'What have we here?' The second man is also dressed in black, but unlike Taylor, he is short and stocky. His voice has a broad Irish brogue. His hairline shows significant receding through the stubble of grey. He is older, with tattooed arms bulging with muscle and a short thick, corded neck.

'Christ Maggie, pull yourself together!' Julian has a pistol digging into his back and it's making him nervous.

Maggie ignores him and leans against the first man. She looks up at him and flutters her lashes. You're very handsome you know, but you smell bad. You need a bath. You can have a bath in my bath if you like. Julian ran me one before, but I'm finished now.

'Christ Maggie.' Panic suffocates Julian and his breath comes in sharp pants. The situation needs assessing and Maggie is behaving as if she might know the men, at least the one she calls Taylor.

She seems unconcerned at the intrusion, flirting with the man at the door. Is it because she's stoned? What a slut. What are they doing here? Who are they? What are they going to do? Julian's mind reels with possibilities. The spot on his back where the pistol points feels enormous and hot, like it's on fire.

The older man prods Julian to move closer to Maggie.

Taylor puts his arms around her, and puts his guess, that she's on ecstasy, to the test. 'Do you love me then darling?'

Maggie looks sideways from under her eyelashes at Julian and back to Taylor. 'I love everyone.' She throws her hands into the air.

Taylor purses his lips, taking in Julian's clothing, noticing the shirt is buttoned to the wrong eyelets. He glances at Maggie, seeing her tee-shirt is inside out, and deduces the obvious. 'Has Julian been a naughty boy, then?'

Maggie giggles. 'Yes,' she says, 'he's been a jolly bad boy, but I love him.' She sings a corrupted line from Elvis's Witchcraft. 'Let me forget him, don't mention his name,' and twirls in a circle. She trips on the edge of the rug and Taylor catches her.

'Hey, I thought you loved me.' He grins as he squeezes her against him.

'Yes you're lovely too, but you smell. When you've had a bath, I'll love you too.'

Maggie pushes Taylor away and wobbles out to the terrace. She plonks herself down at the table and takes a mouthful of congealed pasta. 'I'm thirsty,' she says with her mouth full, and drinks more wine.

The three men watch mesmerised. Julian takes two steps towards the terrace.

'Maggie, don't drink any more wine. Have water if you're thirsty.'

Taylor pushes Julian's chest. 'Leave the girl alone Julian. You've done enough damage.'

Julian feels his control slipping. Panic rises in his throat. Maggie is off her face. He didn't realise how stoned she is. The useless retard of a chemistry student made the pills too strong, stronger than Julian anticipated anyway. Or, perhaps it's the steady flow of vodka he's been feeding her all day, topped off by the wine tonight. The whole scene in front of him is out of his control.

Taylor grins, enjoying Julian's discomfit. He's read the situation accurately and now plays it for his own amusement. 'What's in the wine Julian? Have you been naughtier than Miss Maggie knows? My, my, perhaps I'll have to punish you for her. What d'ya think?' He puts his hand against Julian's chest again, pushing him back towards the gunman. Julian stumbles.

The other man is not amused. He scowls at Taylor and shoves the pistol into Julian's back, prodding him towards a straight-backed dining chair. 'Stop fooking about Blunt.'

Maggie looks at the back-lit tableau in the sitting room beyond the glass doors, and for the first time, sees the pistol. Danger penetrates the haze of fantasy in her mind, and with abrupt awareness, she realises her worst nightmare has come true. The bank robber has found her.

Her reactions are slow and dreamlike as she watches Taylor move towards her. Then her brain kicks into flight mode, and she bolts from her chair and across the terrace. But the adrenalin rush she needs to get away isn't there. Taylor catches her and holds her close as he walks her back to the sitting room.

The second man grabs Maggie by her hair. She screams and struggles as he pushes her onto a dining chair, sobbing. 'I didn't tell, I didn't tell, I promise. Please don't hurt me, I promise, I kept my promise, I didn't tell anyone. They don't know anything. I promise, please don't hurt me.'

'Shudit.' O'Riley says. 'Tie her up,' he orders Taylor.

Julian feels cold despite sweat leaving saturation rings around his armpits. His senses are strung to snapping point as he tries to understand what's happening. He's afraid. He's never been so afraid. Who are these bozos and what are they going to do to him? This doesn't seem like a normal burglary. He looks at Maggie. What's she saying? She seems to know the men, recognises the man with the pistol anyway. What hasn't she told anyone? The slow jazz from his USB stick mocks him as he looks around, trying to assess the situation, looking desperately for deliverance.

Taylor, the younger of the two men is tall, and spare, not a weakling, but not too muscular. Julian thinks he can take him although they are the same height. The second man is more of a worry. He appears in charge, the one issuing orders, the one with a pistol, and the man to fear.

Julian feels the loosening of his bowels and clenches his sphincter. He can't let them see his fear. Maggie can't see him fall apart although she's so stoned, the silly bitch wouldn't even notice. Julian watches her begging for mercy.

'Please mister bank robber, please don't hurt me. I didn't tell, I promise I didn't tell. Why are you here? Please don't hurt me.'

'Shudup bitch!' The man points the pistol at Maggie, and she subsides into hiccoughing silence. Taylor purses his lips, wondering what the story is behind the reference to a bank robber.

10.

Discord

The next morning, Maggie opens her eyes, feeling queasy and cold. Morning sun floods through the sliding doors, and she squints against its light. Ropes, binding her to the chair, cut into her arms. Her legs cry with the torment of pins and needles, and her cheek throbs.

She lifts her head, trying to avoid the searing pain from the crick she's developed. Two metres away, Julian sleeps upright, trussed to another dining chair; his head back, mouth hanging open. Across the room, Taylor sits on a sofa and watches her. She can't see the other man. Mr Capricorn, she called him last night.

The paralysing fear she had felt disappeared with the realisation he wasn't the bank robber, whom she has spent the better part of her life fearing. She is still scared of him, but knowing he is not here to wreak vengeance somehow makes him less of a monster. He's a cruel man, but the younger one, Taylor, doesn't seem as bad.

Last night he'd been kind to her, helping her sip water, and stroking her hair. He asked the other man to let them lie down to sleep, tied up but lying on the carpet. The man said no. He said no to most things asked of him.

Taylor whispered in her ear. They'd be out of her hair as soon as their lift arrived. He had rubbed her shoulders and smoothed the hair back from falling into her eyes. While tears had coursed down her face, he amused himself by interrogating that fear, asking who she was expecting and was there anyone else coming? Why did she call the other man, mister bank robber?

Under his gentle stroking hands and soft questioning, years of constrained dread burst forth in an ecstasy induced confession. It rose up from her soul and vomited from her lips in purging frankness. Taylor played her while she trusted him. He listened with apparent understanding and compassion, nodding encouragement. When she confessed to her greatest shame, he kissed her neck and said, 'it's all right, lots of people wet themselves with terror. None of it's your fault.'

Words had raced from her lips unchecked as Julian looked on in astonishment. Taylor's gentle probing extracted more from her about her experience than the police, the trauma counsellor, or Joe had ever managed. Her nightmares ensured she never forgot the man although she told the police she saw nothing, heard nothing, as she lay face down on the bank floor.

Taylor continued stroking her hair, making hushing noises while she cried. 'You're a good girl, he said. 'You don't need to be afraid.' He flirted with her and put a cushion under her head while the other man talked to someone on the phone.

As dammed anxiety spilled from her, ecstasy laced bravado filled the void. She told Taylor about her premonition that morning. She explained that as a beginner, a novice witch, she had again misinterpreted the warning.

Practicing Wicca had helped her cope through the last year as her twins went away to university. She had learned to cast small spells of protection for her children. She told him her grandmother had come to her twice in warning, and again in séance.

The other man's head jerked up when she said séance, but lost interest when she said she hadn't understood the warning. Stung by his dismissal and still not knowing his name she called him Mr Capricorn, sure she was right in her guess of his birth sun, taunting him with threats she'd cast a spell on him if he didn't untie her.

Taylor said, 'do you know my sign too then darling?'

'Sagittarius,' she said without hesitation.

Mr Capricorn continued to ignore her until she said she would summon the dead in séance. Then he turned back to stare at her. She saw fearful curiosity flash across his face as she teased him about summoning the people he had killed.

Taylor's glance flashed between Maggie and Mr Capricorn reading the signs, and he leaned over to Maggie to whisper. 'It's his mother, and if you don't shut up, he will make me hurt you.'

Maggie couldn't stop. Her mouth seemed to have taken on a will of its own. She blathered on about Mr Capricorn's evil deeds and the stories his victims could tell. That was when he got up from his chair, made the sign of the cross and hit her with a backhand, his knuckles catching her cheek bone.

Maggie had subsided into sobbing hiccups until she drifted into fitful dose.

Now, in the early morning light, she turns her head to see if Mr Capricorn is on the other sofa behind her. Her cheek throbs with the movement, but she can't see him. She whispers to Taylor, 'I'm thirsty.' Her voice croaks and she clears it.

Taylor gets off the sofa and walks towards her. 'Shhh,' he says, his hand cupping her mouth as he bends down to whisper in her ear. 'Brendan's asleep, don't wake him.' He checks to make sure she's understood before he takes his hand from her mouth. The smell of shampoo and the musky sweet scent of Joe's aftershave tells Maggie he's used her bathroom to shower.

'I'm thirsty,' she whispers again.

He comes back with a glass of water, which he holds to her lips as he strokes her hair. She drinks, and he kisses her neck when she's had enough. She flinches, repulsed by his touch.

He smiles, whispering in her ear, 'last night you said you would love me if I showered. Well I'm showered now.'

She drops her eyes as blood surges up her neck and stains her cheeks. God, what has she done? She was so pissed. She hadn't drunk that much since, since... Well, ever that she can remember.

Memories of her abandonment to Julian flood into her mind and guilt regurgitates in bilious remorse. God what will Joe do? He can't know. He won't ever forgive her.

She casts a venomous look at Julian as she remembers how he went out of his way to seduce her. He forced too much wine on her, she wasn't herself. Guilt loops in her head, and leaks from her eyes as she wriggles through blame and possible scapegoats, but Maggie knows she is the one at fault.

Taylor misinterprets her tears, and strokes her hair. 'You need not be frightened of me, little Maggie.'

She says nothing. She should be more frightened, but somehow the terror she should feel, isn't there. Taylor won't hurt her although Mr Capricorn—Brendan, is another matter.

Taylor watches her struggle, her pupils still enlarged from the effects of the drugs. He can see she wants to lash out at him, obliterating her remorse in battle. His smile is rapacious as he reads the guilt in her eyes. Running his finger down her neck to her cleavage, he can smell fear, mixed with the stale smell of sex and it excites him, but a sound behind him has him back on the sofa within seconds.

Brendan coughs and snorts, regurgitating phlegm. The sofa squeaks as he rises. He goes to the terrace where he spits out a great gob onto the lawn then stands scratching his groin. Tendrils of morning mist weave between hill peaks and along valleys above streams and rivers, raggedly catching on trees, to drift through air washed clean with last night's rain.

He unzips his fly and urinates on the lawn, then walks over to the terrace table, pistol clutched in his hand. He jerks his head for Taylor to join him and clears the table with a sweep of his forearm. Flies and beetles rise into the air as last night's dinner dishes shatter on the tiled terrace.

They sit at the table, and Brendan stares into the sitting room at his captives. He's worried. Their contact hadn't shown at the rendezvous point two days ago. He promised; gave his word that the local Chapter would arrange everything necessary once the money was safely delivered.

Brendan arranged the money through his own Chapter so he's sure it would have been delivered on time. The trouble is that they are from rival outfits, but a promise is a promise, and they said they could get him and Taylor back to Sydney, but the bastard hadn't shown.

Brendan will make him regret that, but for now he is worried about how they will get out of this God forsaken dump. The farm isn't part of their plan and it complicates matters. Hostages are always a bad idea, despite the farm being a good bolthole. They had to have somewhere to hide from the Filth until he could get things sorted. The Yankee bloke inside, and that blathering slanger are complications he wants gone.

Taylor persuaded him it wasn't a good idea. He reasoned their crime was merely breaking out from Remand, stealing a vehicle, and a firearm. If they added murder, it became another matter entirely. The cops resources are strained anyway, but a murder charge would see those resources found. At least this place is a relatively safe haven to rest and plan the next move.

Brendan's lower eyelid twitches as he thinks of their plans going haywire. He presses his finger against it to stop the tic. He isn't like Taylor, who is emotionless. It makes him a highly effective member of the Chapter when he bothers to follow orders, but with Taylor, women always cause problems.

'Ruled by his bellend,' Brendan said, blaming Taylor for stopping at the Pub where they were caught. The fooking ballbeg wanted to stop because he heard the barmaid was a goer and he needed a shag.

Brendan disapproves. The way he carries on with women is

almost as bad as being a rapist. Brendan can't abide rapists. They, along with serial killers, drug addicts and paedophiles, turn his stomach. There's something untrustworthy about such people, unwholesome. Killing isn't the problem if you do it clean. Killing for business reasons, Brendan understands. Nothing wrong there, but the rest is a disgusting perversion of weak minds, to his way of thinking.

Taylor knows how Brendan views his seduction of women. The way he persists until he gets his way no matter how long it takes or what he has to do for it. He says it's not rape, but Brendan's not so sure. It sounds like a technicality to him.

Worry consumes Brendan; it always has. It rules his life. In fact, nothing has gone right since he and Taylor came up to North Queensland to collect the firearms, delivered by way of Cape York from Papua New Guinea, and he suspects a double cross.

He often wonders if worrying about things going wrong, actually has a kind of mysterious cosmic force that makes them go wrong. 'Worrying invites the devil into your life,' is what his mother told him. God rest her soul. Brendan crosses himself. She said it was his incessant worrying that drove her husband away although Brendan wasn't sad to see the back of the violent bastard. He didn't touch the drink himself now, or drugs, but he knew with certainty it was his fault he lost both his parents.

The Nuns at the orphanage told him he should instead worry over the state of his immortal soul, so he dutifully worried about that too. On All Hallows night, he hid shaking under his threadbare blanket, clutching red berries to keep the witches at bay as the souls of the dead crossed the portal of the great earthly divide. Memories of his Ma's stories of witches and hob-goblins plagued his imagination

He snivelled out the words of prayers with his eyes screwed tight shut as he bargained with God, to save him from the evil ones who would steal his soul. The red berries worked, or at least he had never seen a witch or goblin. Now, he doesn't think he has a soul. That woman inside claimed to be a witch so killing her would be a service.

Taylor leans back in his chair, his face expressionless. Behind the bland facade, he feels pity for poor old Brendan. The pity he has for a beautiful butterfly as he pulls off its wings, squashing the remaining wingless slug in disgust. Brendan is like a wingless slug, not that the poor bloke had ever been beautiful. Someone should put him out of his misery, but the code is the code and it would never be Taylor doing the deed, not unless instructed anyway. Taylor respects the code, but sometimes Brendan's orders need ignoring. His incessant worrying and fear of risk got them into this trouble in the first place.

He watches the surreptitious flick of the wrist as Brendan makes the sign of the cross. As far as Taylor is concerned, Brendan's reverence for God is superstition, and he doesn't believe in luck, superstitions or God. Taylor believes in himself. If Brendan took greater risks or was more flexible it wouldn't be so bad, but he dithers. If Taylor were by himself, he wouldn't still be here. It was sticking with the brother that caused the problems. The bloke's weak, but he is a brother, and in charge.

Brendan once told Taylor about his worry theory that he had driven his father away and killed his mother. Taylor didn't laugh. Most of the brothers had sad, brutal stories to tell. Taylor was one of the few from a wealthy background, privileged, but perverted by his too affectionate mother. Taylor smiles as he thinks of his father, still in gaol for her murder. Bastard deserves the time. He never looked out for Taylor.

Maggie strains to hear their low voices as Brendan makes the sign of the cross. He catches her eavesdropping, and stares at her with protruding pale eyes, his nose mashed against his face, and his jowls dragging thin lips down at the corners. 'Food! You,' he says pointing at Maggie, 'get us breakfast and coffee, lots of it.' He gestures to Taylor, 'untie her and watch her. No maggotin about.'

Maggie stands up, rubbing her arms and flexing her toes to get her circulation back. Julian is awake, and she opens her mouth to speak to him.

'Shud ye gob.' Brendan orders.

She walks down the corridor, Taylor behind her. As soon as they enter the kitchen, he grabs her, spinning her around, pulling her into his chest, and kissing her hard. She struggles as he turns her facing away, holding her around the waist, her bottom pulled back against his hips. He kisses her neck as he fiddles with his belt buckle.

A door slams and Taylor lets her go. No sound is uttered as Maggie hurries to the fridge. She's terrified, but doesn't know what to do, so she does nothing, pretending nothing happened. If she ignores it, perhaps it will go away.

He hovers, watching her get bacon from the small fridge freezer, placing it in the microwave to defrost. Maggie grinds coffee beans and puts bread into the toaster as bacon sizzles in the pan.

'I will have to feed the chickens and let them out of their coup,' she says.

'After breakfast, we'll see. You're quite a little goer aren't you? What were you on last night—ecstasy? That Yank, Julian—he's not your husband. Where is your husband?'

Maggie stops stock still, an uncracked egg poised above the bowl. The bastard! It makes sense now, her behaviour, and the feelings of intense emotion. Ecstasy. Oh Jesus. She tries to regain her composure, marshalling a bland expression on her face.

'What's up gorgeous, cat got your tongue?'

She stares at Taylor. 'Scrambled eggs okay?'

'Yeah.' He walks over, putting his arms around her, holding her body close while he rubs his groin against her bottom and kisses her neck. She tries to ignore him, continuing to break eggs into the bowl.

'Don't,' she says controlling her fear. The urge to scream and run is overwhelming, but she needs to use her head. 'I can't cook with you doing that, and Brendan wouldn't like his food burned.' He stops. She's right, he's afraid of Brendan.

He chuckles. 'You're one hot momma, you are. I can wait. We have plenty of time.' He walks over and sits on a bar stool at the kitchen counter, watching her as she moves about the kitchen.

'Who are you Taylor, I mean what are you doing here? I have a little money in my purse, but not much. You can take anything you want. I won't tell anyone if you just go, and don't hurt us.'

'That's nice of you darlin, but we will stay for a while. Of course, I intend to take what I want while I'm here, get my drift?' He looks at her meaningfully.

Maggie shudders. The hangover, of what she now knows is the residual drug, along with alcohol in her system, makes her calmer than she would be normally. She has to get out, look for an opportunity to escape. If she can get to the forest, they won't find her, but she'd lose her way. Where can she run? The neighbours are too far away. They would catch her before she got up the road.

Perhaps she can get to the phone extension in the bedroom, she can hang up on the person at the other end and then phone the police. That will take too long, but maybe if she can grab her mobile and run to the top of the road she'll get a signal and call for help. How will she make Taylor relax his vigilance so she can bolt? She walks towards the kitchen door.

'Where're you going?'

'I need to get something from the pantry.'

'What d'ya need? I'll get it.'

'Salt.'

'There's salt on the bench.'

'Oh!'

'Common Maggie, don't play games. You're a good girl. Do as you're told and you'll be all right. Don't make Brendan angry. I won't be able to protect you and that would be a shame; pretty little thing like you.'

Maggie feels defeated, her mind still foggy. She needs to bide her time, pretend she's complying and await her chance. Taylor's guarded, and she needs him to relax.

'Common darlin, talk to me. You're Maggie; that much I know. What's your surname?'

'Williams.'

'And your husband – what's his name?'

'None of your business.'

'No? Seems like Mr. Williams will want to know what you were up to last night. I might just be the one to tell him.'

'Doctor.'

'What?'

'Doctor, my husband is not Mr. Williams, he's Doctor Williams.' Maggie wonders why she insists on his honorific. She's bothered by this thug calling Joe, Mr. She is proud of being Dr. William's wife, but it's an odd conundrum wanting this thug to know her husband is a doctor of philosophy, especially as Taylor knows she cheated on him last night. Anger at Julian and her own guilt surges in her throat, but she pushes the thoughts away. Her brain is not up to it. Focus Maggie, she tells herself.

'Where is he then, this Dr. Williams?'

Maggie ignores him. She puts the bacon and eggs on plates, pours coffee, and arranges the food on a tray. She glances at Taylor, waiting for him to carry the tray, but he smiles as if he can read her mind.

'You take it.'

She shrugs and picks up the tray to take to the sitting room, walking in front of him. The opportunity to crash it over his head, and bolt out the door is lost.

In the sitting room, Brendan is still on the phone. Julian is tied to his chair. Taylor points to the coffee table and Maggie lays down the tray.

'Feed him,' he orders pointing at Julian and takes a plate over to Brendan. Then he takes his own plate to the sofa.

Julian squirms. 'Untie me so I can eat by myself.'

Taylor concentrates on his food. 'No.'

Brendan stops his conversation and pushes the phone mouthpiece against his chest. He glowers as if Julian is making too much noise. For a minute, his stare remains solid, frightening Maggie who watches the pistol, clutched in his meaty hand. It dangles between his knees. The plate of food, in front of him, remains untouched.

Maggie picks up a plate of bacon and eggs for Julian who shakes his head. She ignores him, not wanting to feed him, but angry at him for giving her drugs before seducing her. The kernel of an idea formulates in her foggy brain as she cuts his food into bite-sized pieces. With her back to Brendan and Taylor, she crams food into his mouth, and hisses, 'you drugged me you revolting specimen. You drugged me and took advantage.'

She reads acknowledgement on Julian's face as he flashes a glance across at Brendan. While he chews, she mouths, 'where are they?'

He frowns.

'Where are the drugs?'

His gaze once more flicks to Brendan engaged on the phone, and then across to Taylor, engrossed in his food, and shakes his head.

'Tell me you bastard, or I'll tell them you're trying to escape.'

He swallows. 'Soap bag, bathroom,' he mutters.

Maggie finishes feeding Julian in silence, pushing food against his teeth, poking the fork into his lips, barely restraining herself from stabbing him harder. She is angrier with him than with the criminals. He's ruined everything. How can she face her husband again? How will she face her children? A sense of bitter betrayal settles her fear.

11.

Guilt

Joe awakes to the repetitive burbling chorus of Chowchillas' penetrating his consciousness. He rolls onto his back and takes stock of his surroundings. His head hurts, and his bones ache with the chill of damp earth seeping through the ground sheet.

Outside he hears the women's voices and sits up with a groan, head pounding as he waits for the nausea and wooziness to abate. Visions from yesterday creep into his mind. He puts his head in his hands, thinking oh, fuck, fuck. What's he going to do? Maggie will be out of her mind with worry. Oh Christ, how is he going to explain this? She can't know. Is this it, has he killed his marriage?

An image of Lexi steals into his mind. Is that what he wants? After all he and Maggie have been through together, is this just an unconscious desire to sabotage his marriage so he can be free? Does he want freedom? Sadness leaves him feeling empty. He loves Maggie, and it dawns on him, he never wanted to jeopardise his marriage. Lexi, the German backpackers, the longing for freedom; perhaps it was all just a fantasy. Ah shit, what does he know? Perhaps it's better not to dwell on these things.

He eases out of the tent to stand in the sun. The women swim naked, and he wonders if a morning swim in cold water will help his hangover. He stretches and strips off his clothes, spreading them on a sunny rock, and wades in, ducking his head, and gasping with shock as he surfaces from the cold water.

They laugh.

His head clears and he smiles, knowing he should say something, but not knowing what. In the end he says, 'thank you.'

It sounds daft to him, but Brigitte responds. 'It's our pleasure.'

Tatjana merely smiles.

'I have to go. My wife will worry.'

'Yes, we will take you.'

'No! Ah—I don't think that's wise, do you?'

'Oh, yes it's fine. We will take you, and we meet your wife. We stay at your house tonight, then tomorrow we go. It's good, yes? We are not saying anything about yesterday. We just wish to see where you live and make a visit, have hot bath, some food, wash clothes, find some comfort.'

Joe feels alarm rising. 'My wife will be upset that I didn't get home last night. She may have called the police. They may have a search party out looking for me.'

Brigitte laughs. 'You will tell her you are lost and we find. We're your saviour, no?'

Joe stares at her. It might just work. What choice does he have? Guilt about yesterday, the sex the drugs, not going home, worrying people unnecessarily, all clash in his muddled head. He wonders if Maggie has called the police. Christ, what a mess. She has probably called the parents and the children too. Everyone will in a stew with worry. They might already have search parties out scouring the country. Maybe, pretending he was lost, and that these women found him is a good idea, despite the blow to his pride.

'Okay, but I can't let her know about, about.... Um.'

Brigitte laughs. 'The sex, it was good, no?'

'No. I mean yes, it was good, but it was wrong, my wife... I love my wife.' Joe trails off, realising it's true. He loves Maggie, and if she finds out, she won't forgive him.

'Pheff! It was just sex, not love. It doesn't matter.'

'Yes, but she can't know.'

'Okay,' Brigitte shrugs. 'You want to have sex now?'

'Christ no! Ah sorry—I mean thank you, but I can't.'

'Okay,' Brigitte shrugs again, her nipples tight in the cold water.

Joe stares at the naked women in front of him. Guilt and desire churn in his gut, struggling for dominance, but he turns away and swims to the waterfall, thinking, I can't! I can't say I am stoned now. Not that being stoned constitutes an excuse. He needs space to get himself under control.

He searches for frogs among the rocks at the base of the falls, moving his thoughts to the mundane, and calls the women over, avoiding looking at their naked breasts, and their round bottoms as they bend over to get a better view.

The frogs cling to the underside of a rocky outcrop and he explains their endangered status. 'That's why the waterfall has to remain secret, for the frogs' protection.'

The women nod. All he hopes is they will not draw a map to the place for every backpacker in Australia.

Half an hour later, their camp packed, they walk along an old logging track until they find the hired van, parked on a side road off the main highway. Brigitte drives, and Tatjana sits between her and Joe, her warm thigh pressing against his. For a moment, he allows fantasy to claim his imagination, dreaming of being young again without a care; without responsibilities, without guilt. He fantasises about travelling with them, going on to the next camp, never going home. He could just disappear.

Get a grip, he chides himself. You need to have your story straight when you get home. He devises scenarios in his mind. Creating one after another, seeing the holes and then discarding them. Eventually, he arrives at bare plausibility. He'll tell Maggie he was late arriving at the waterfall, because he went off course in the forest with his sat nav running out of battery, and stayed at the waterfall for the night so as not to lose his way home in the dark.

He'll claim he met the two women this morning as they came looking for the waterfall, and show indignation at the twin's indiscretion about its location, but he will be grateful and beholden to them for agreeing to drive him home. Yes that will work. The least Maggie can do to thank them is give them a bed for a night. Shit, he remembers the twins and the parents arrive to night, it will be a full house. Lucky, Maggie won't have time to interrogate him. It's not brilliant or very imaginative, but it will have to do.

He explains his story to the women. They seem indifferent to his predicament, asking why he needs to say they weren't there last night. Brigitte shrugs and agrees. Tatjana frowns and nods, but he's compelled to explain his reasoning to the women. He doesn't want them judging him, but there's no sane reason, except to say he doesn't want his wife to know he cheated on her. Isn't that enough?

It sounds like a poor excuse even to his ears; a coward's excuse. He knows some men have affairs all the time. That fellow in the Law faculty is notorious for it, but Joe's never cheated. What about Lexi a voice in his head says? No, it's not fair. He never did anything but chat with Lexi, and yesterday was meaningless, just sex not love as Brigitte says. He wants to get away with it, not to pay what might be an unacceptable price for cheating.

Maggie won't forgive him, he knows that. What will his kids say? His son will look at him with scorn, disappointed in his pathetic old dad. His daughter will vent her disgust, loudly and often. He doesn't want Brigitte and Tatjana to think badly of him either. Although, he's not sure why he cares when he won't see them again after tonight. He just wants respect, not to be viewed as a pathetic, randy old goat, a dirty old man.

Maggie will have called the police by now. How long will she have waited? Did she wait until the morning, not wanting to disturb them at night? That would be so like her. Never mind, her husband is bleeding his life blood onto the mouldering leaf litter of the forest or writhing in agony from a snake bite; mustn't worry the poor policeman at night time.

Joe gives vent to anger to ease his culpability as he imagines Maggie's indifference to his plight and thinks I bet she didn't even notice I wasn't there. She rarely notices if I'm in bed with her or not, what would be different last night.

Will the police interview the German women? Why would they need to do that? No, he is sure they won't, but nagging doubt persists. He's not good at lying. Maggie can read him like a book. Will Brigitte and Tatjana stick to the story if the police are involved? They certainly wouldn't mention drugs, but they might say they were there last night. He wishes he had his mobile, at least he'd get a signal on the highway, and phoning ahead would give him advanced warning.

By the time they reach the farm, Joe's lips are bruised and sore from squeezing and tugging. Brigitte stops the car in the middle of the driveway. Lorikeets squabble in the branches above, fighting over the red and gold flowers of the Black Bean.

'Keep going,' Joe says. 'There's a gravelled bit further along next to the house... Wait! On second thoughts, this will be fine. Park here, and I'll go ahead to speak with Maggie before you come in.'

Joe looks away as Brigitte raises an eyebrow. Tatjana says something in German and they laugh. He knows they're talking about him and his fear at confronting his wife. What if the Cops are here? He needs time to sort this out before the women arrive at the house; one thing at a time. 'Take your time and come up to the house when you're ready. I'll just get things organised.'

Joe hurries along the driveway and across the gravelled parking area next to the house, leaving the women to sort out their stuff in the van. A utility truck is parked on the gravel next to Julian's car. It doesn't look like a police vehicle. Perhaps the neighbours have come to help. The smell of bacon frying assails Joe's senses as he walks towards the house. Indignation whips away trepidation, as he thinks, Jesus she's cooking bacon for the whole neighbourhood.

Self-righteous anger mounts until he finds the laundry, garage and front doors all locked. It's odd, they never lock the house. Caution takes over as he walks around the side of the house and across the lawn to the kitchen door. Wet grass squelches under his feet as he imagines the scene in the kitchen; people sitting around scoffing bacon and eggs talking about sending out a search party. He imagines their surprise as he walks in, their exchanged glances as the German women walk in behind him.

Christ, he'll look a fool. They'll all know. Maggie will know. He slows, placing his feet softly, as he approaches the kitchen and looks in through the window. The room is empty and relief floods through him.

Frying pans on the sink are evidence of the bacon and eggs she has cooked. He steps onto the back porch and turns the door handle, but this door is locked as well. 'What the hell is going on?'

He walks around the corner and steps onto the terrace where he can see diagonally into the sitting room through the sliding doors. A stranger sits at the desk, his body side-on to Joe, the phone pressed against his ear. Joe's mouth waters at the sight of the untouched bacon and eggs on the desk, until he sees the pistol dangling between the man's knees. What's this?

He flattens his body against the wall as he tries to comprehend the situation. That bloke doesn't look like a police officer. He looks like a thug, and where is Maggie? Someone moves, scraping a chair, alerting the man on the phone, who glances up before turning back to his conversation. Maggie walks into Joe's view as she carries a plate to the coffee table. No one talks except the man on the phone, and his voice is too low for Joe to hear.

'Hellooo, where are you?' Brigitte skips around the side of the house.

He signals for her to keep quiet with his finger held to his lips.

She looks puzzled. 'What is it?'

Her eyes widened as Brendan steps out through the sliding doors, pistol pointing at them. Joe hears a scream from around the house, and a few moments later another man comes around the corner pushing Tatjana ahead of him, her arm twisted behind her back, her face shocked and twisted in pain.

Confusion tinged with uncertainty and fear makes Joe's tone pompous. 'Who are you, what are you doing here, and where is my wife?'

'Ah, the doctor has arrived,' Taylor grins. 'Inside with you now. Your lovely wife is in the lounge.'

Brendan gestures with the pistol for Joe to go through the sitting room doors.

Taylor says, 'quite a little party we're gathering.' He pushes the round-eyed Tatjana along behind a confused Brigitte. 'I must say, Dr. Williams, you do hang with the prettiest women.'

12.

Fortitude

'Come on you lot, we won't make it before dark, unless you get a scoot on.'

Stan leans against the balcony rail, looking east over the sea, the salt breeze flapping his loose shirt. It's a shame Maggie and Joe hadn't come to the Island yesterday. He had been looking forward to it. He quite likes his son-in-law although he is beginning to suspect the man could do with growing a bit of backbone, letting his wife's neuroses rule their lives.

Ah well, he's probably lucky. The bloke is a relatively decent sort and looks after Maggie and his grandchildren although Miss Abby is getting a bit ahead of herself, demanding he calls her Abigail. He isn't going to start now by calling her something other than what he's always called her. No matter how much she sulks or puts on airs and graces.

He smiles remembering her excitement yesterday afternoon. She wasn't such a little miss when they came across the whale pod with the baby. She shrieked and jabbered like a small girl. That was more like his granddaughter. She's still a kid, no matter how old and grown up she pretends to be.

Maggie, now she's a different story. He doesn't know what's wrong with her. She's changed. When did it become too inconvenient for her to visit her old Dad? Elaine said something about bad dreams. The world's gone crazy. People can't travel when they have bad dreams?

He doesn't get it. She's been weird since they moved north, after that bank holdup incident. Well, he told Elaine not to let Maggie go to Sydney in the first place. Why she couldn't attend the local dance academy, he doesn't know.

Still, he knows bank holdups are terrifying ordeals for the victims. His police training taught him that, but the holdup was eighteen years ago, for God's sake. Still his language was regrettably choice when his wife said they weren't coming.

'Don't blaspheme dear,' Elaine said in her firm, unflappable way. 'You never will understand your daughter. Just let it go.'

He still smarts at that criticism, but she may have a point. He understands men all right. It's women who are the mystery, but damn-it he was looking forward to their visit. A spot of fishing with Joe and Paul would've been the ticket. He'd let the women go shopping or whatever it is that fills their time.

That's another mystery—he has never worked out what Elaine does all day. She's always busy, but with what, he has no idea. It's not like she works; never had a job in her life. Stan wonders if that's a mistake. Perhaps she set a bad example for Maggie. Would a job cure her neurosis?

That's what everyone says now. People have to get a job, get engaged and feel they're contributing. Bullshit in Stan's view, and he said that when the women in town asked him to volunteer for the ambulance committee.

He has enough to do fishing thank you, but perhaps that's because he has something to fill his time. Now the twins are off Maggie's hands perhaps she needs something to occupy her, not those wombats who think they're witches; what next! He tentatively suggested Maggie should go out to work, when he learned about her depression diagnosis, even though he thought it all new age hogwash, but he's willing to be proved wrong.

Maggie looked all right at the mid semester break. She didn't seem sick or anything, and Stan said at the time, he wasn't sure he believed in depression. Being sad he understood. When his mother died he had been sad. Sadness is normal and one gets over it, but being sad because your kids leave home for a while, well that's beyond Stan.

In his opinion, Maggie should have been delighted, but she went to pieces. She just needs to pull herself together and get on with things instead of moping about all day. Depression, it seems like another one of those new-fangled things. Like not travelling when you have bad dreams. What a lot of nonsense. Joe needs to take his wife in hand. He always warned Elaine that Maggie was spoilt.

He's not convinced working actually fixes things either. In his day, wives didn't go to work, unless it was necessary. They were too busy looking after their men and their homes. That's a woman's proper work. Not like now where women demand a career like men. Who looks after the house while they're at work, he wants to know.

Women's working patterns are probably directly correlated with the increase in crime statistics. He will lay money on it. No one home to tend the children, latch door key kids getting into trouble, houses standing empty, an invitation for any petty thieves to help themselves.

Abby's another one who wants a career. Daft girl! She should find a good man and settle down before she gets too old. His Elaine was never interested, or not that he knew about anyway. She made her career looking after him and Maggie. Anyway, in the early days, it would have been impossible for her to hold down a job of any kind with all their moving from station to station. Latterly, he supposes, she might have found something part-time in the City somewhere. Stan looks at his watch.

'What are you doing in there, Elaine? Aren't you ready yet?'

His wife's voice floats down the hallway. 'Have another coffee dear, we'll be along shortly.'

Stan walks inside to pour another coffee. He doesn't need a second invitation. It's funny; usually she tells him he has too much caffeine, calls him an addict. Silly goose, she wouldn't know an addict if one fell into her lap.

Stan knew plenty of addicts in his time, or at least he had put them in gaol. Addicts and drunks, the scourge of society; he takes his coffee out to the balcony, sipping appreciatively while looking over the ruffled Coral Sea.

The day is clear, perfect for fishing. The sky is that intense blue he swears only ever happens around these parts, unlike the drizzly damp of the southern Tablelands where he is being forced to spend the next few days.

He doesn't know why Joe didn't buy a house near him and Elaine instead of that weed-infested block. He thinks, farm my foot, load of old scrub that needs clearing. It probably harbours all sorts of unsavoury critters, Dingos, feral pigs, snakes, spiders, weeds and more than likely, some addled hippy's drug plot. They even had tree snakes living in the eaves of the house for Christ sakes, and frogs are always taking up residence in their toilets.

He doesn't relish spending time there. It's too far from the sea, with no fishing unless you can count the river. Stan doesn't. Anyway, it's sure to be wet; guaranteed, but at least he can see for himself what's going on with Maggie. Something is causing the problems.

Depression doesn't run in his family so it must be in Joe's although how that affects Maggie he isn't sure. Perhaps it's something Joe's doing wrong. Elaine said Maggie is better now because of her friendship with the wombat. Baloney! How can a person have this so called depression, an illness that requires medication, then, poof—like that, get over it? He snaps his fingers and glances around, embarrassed in case anyone's watching.

There's still no sign of Elaine and the twins. What's taking them so long? He sighs, knowing from experience, there's no hurrying her. Pity Maggie doesn't take after her mother, calm unflappable and organised. Elaine never burdens Stan with her emotions.

He stops, and contemplates that fact, then mutters, 'come to think of it, I don't know what Elaine thinks or feels most of the time. The old girl's so practical; she doesn't seem to suffer girly emotions.'

Maggie's problems certainly don't come from Elaine, but to recover magically because she has nice new friends—well, Stan doesn't quite buy that either. Either Maggie was ill with depression or she had never had it. He suspects the latter. She needs a firm hand. He'll have a quiet word to Joe about standing up to that wife of his, putting his foot down firmly.

Stan rubs his chest. His indigestion is giving him gyp again. He gazes out at the white caps washing up the sandy beach. Yep, that's what's needed, a quiet talk man to man. Joe needs to stiffen his resolve. This business of cancelling holiday plans at the last minute and getting him and Elaine to pick up the kids is weird.

Not that he minds. He loves the kids and having them to stay is always good. It isn't the drive he minds either. Stan is used to driving. It's only four hours, four and a half if they stop, and they will need to stop. Joe never has any beer in the house, or nothing any sane man could call beer. That fancy piss-weak stuff he stocks is just lolly water. They'll have to stop at the bottle'O on the way. He'll need a beer when they arrive, if they ever leave. At this rate they won't be there before dark.

'Right ho you lot, ready or not we're off.' Stan walks indoors as Elaine walks out with Paul behind her.

'Take the suitcases down to the car, and then come back and help your sister,' Elaine says to Paul who pulls a face, but obliges. She turns to Stan. 'Will you wash your cup dear?'

He washes his cup and empties the coffee pot, rinsing it and putting it upside down on the sink. He never minds helping Elaine, and it'll get them out of the house quicker if he helps. He closes the French doors to the balcony and checks doors and windows around the house.

It's Magnetic Island and they are unlikely to have a break and enter, but one can't take chances, especially with the prison escapees at large. He has memorised the number of the stolen Ute, and he'll keep an eye out for it on their journey north. That would be a turn up for the books; retired Cop nabs escaped crims. That would show the young fellows.

Elaine's voice drifts up the stairs. 'Come along dear, we're waiting for you.'

13.

Wrath

At the sound of a woman's voice calling hallo, Brendan and Taylor stare at each other in silence. Brendan lowers the phone to the desk and nods to Taylor. In three strides, he crosses the room to duck through the glass doors, holding his pistol in front of him. Taylor runs silently down the hallway towards the laundry door.

Maggie glances at the phone. He didn't hang up, so someone is still on the other end. Can she ring for help? No, she won't have time. She sprints in bare feet after Taylor.

As he lets himself out of the laundry door, she slips into the guest bathroom and rummages through Julian's soap bag. She isn't sure what she's looking for, but finds a small plastic packet of pills, three white ones and four that are a bluish colour.

'The bastard,' she says again, indignation swelling at his duplicity, and pushes the packet into her shorts pocket. She opens the door a crack to peek out into the hallway. It's all clear, so she runs to the kitchen and turns on the sink taps.

Taylor stomps in. 'What the fuck do you think you are playing at?' He grabs her arm.

'Ouch, that hurts. I was just cleaning up.'

'Leave it.' He turns off the taps and drags her towards the sitting room. 'Your husband's home. Make a wrong move, and he hears all about your shenanigans last night with your little boyfriend.' He smirks. 'Mind you, with the two lovely lasses he has in tow, he might not care.'

Maggie wonders what he's saying. Joe should have the twins with him. He drags her to the sitting room. A dishevelled Joe stands in front of Brendan's pistol. The look of relief in his face as he sees Maggie makes her want to cry.

'Joe,' she wrenches her arm from Taylor's grip, and runs to him.

His arms fold around her. 'Maggie, are you all right? Christ, I'm sorry.'

'Me too.' She clings to him, burying her face against his chest.

Realisation, that she only has herself to blame, washes over her. For eighteen years, she did everything possible to ensure her family's safety, and she failed. Not only did she fail to keep them safe, but her premonition ensured they would be in the most perilous place possible. To cap it off, she betrayed Joe. Her attempt to control every situation, and forecast every risk to her family's safety, has backfired horribly.

She shakes her head. 'I'm so sorry, it's all my fault.'

'No Maggie, it's not. It's me, it's my fault.' Guilt and self-condemnation burn his eyelids as he thinks of his betrayal while she faced peril from the very thing she warned him about, and which he had not believed.

Taylor wrenches her away. 'How sweet. You're both sorry. Now what for, I wonder? Stow it. Maggie, go join the girls on the sofa.'

For the first time Maggie notices the two women huddled on the sofa, and she looks up into Joe's face, but he looks away.

Taylor says, 'Dr. Williams, if you will just take a seat on this chair, I'll make you more comfortable.' He points to the dining chair, trying to look nonchalant, but he's worried.

There are too many of them. He needs to get them under control fast while they're still frightened and confused. One pistol won't keep order if they're free to act, particularly the Williams fellow. Taylor knows the type. He'll risk everything for Maggie. He's one of those lunatic self-sacrificing heroes.

Joe remains with his arms around Maggie. 'What's going on, who are you—what're you doing in my house?' Indignant and confused, he looks to Julian for answers. 'Julian, what's going on?'

Taylor pulls Maggie away from Joe, pushing her onto the couch with the other two women. He stands back looking at the three of them. 'Nice little harem you have Dr. Williams; think I might sample some of the delicacies while I am here.'

Brigitte rises. 'We are just giving Joe a lift. We will go now.'

Taylor pushes her back onto the sofa. 'Hm, German girls. Where did you find these lovelies Dr. Williams?'

Brigitte tries to stand again, and he snaps, 'stay where you are.' She shrinks back against Tatjana.

'Stop muckin about Taylor. Tie 'em up.' Brendan looks grumpy. He hates Taylor's theatrics. 'Fook, what is this place. Any more likely to turn up?' He asks the question rhetorically, gazing around the room as if an answer might materialise.

Taylor leans towards Brendan, saying something in a low voice.

'Fook, find some then.' Brandon waves the pistol at Maggie. 'Take her. I'll watch this lot. Hurry, and no muckin about.'

Taylor nods. 'Get up.' He says to Maggie. 'Where do you keep your rope?'

'We don't have any.'

'Bullshit, this is a farm isn't it? Of course you have rope, or tie wire or something.'

'Maggie, there's rope in the garage, just show him.' Joe's worried. Now isn't the time for defiance, not until they have a plan. He doesn't want them to hurt her.

Taylor pushes Maggie before him towards the corridor that leads to the garage. Joe's stomach lurches as he sees Maggie's wide frightened eyes looking back at him from the doorway. He can't protect her. She needed him, and he let her down, drinking, smoking and screwing while she's going through hell, and he wasn't here for her. The one time she needed him. He corrects himself. The second time she needed him, really needed him, and he's failed both times.

No wonder she rejects him. He's a useless, pathetic self-centred mediocre man, who can't even take care of his wife. An urge to do something swamps him. His brain stops assessing and planning. He stops thinking. The thin veneer of logic slips aside as he leaps at Brendan.

Brendan's body is all hard muscle, but Joe has the advantage of greater height, surprise and forward propulsion, which carries them backwards into Julian, still tied to his chair.

Something sharp catches Julian's cheek bone, and he jerks his head as the chair topples to the tiled floor. Brendan and Joe fall on top of him as he lies dazed. Fury mounts at his helplessness.

Brendan rolls off and tries to stand. Joe lunges again, knocking him to the floor, and hanging onto his legs as the pistol skids away. Brendan scrambles after the gun, veins budging in his temples as he pulls himself and Joe along the floor.

From the hallway, Taylor, hears Julian shout and runs back to the sitting room. He scoops up the pistol and presses the barrel against the crown of Joe's head. Before it's even started, it's finished. Taylor stands, one boot pressing Joe to the floor.

Joe slumps. If only he had been faster. If only he had waited until Taylor got to the garage. He's blown it by acting on impulse too soon. They'll be on guard now, and he won't get another chance.

Brendan gets up, pulls his jacket straight and walks towards Joe to take a swing with his boot. Too late, Joe sees the foot coming, and jerks out the way. Pain explodes in his head, and his vision darkens. Crackling streaks of blue, red and silver light sizzle as his neck jerks backwards.

Pain and confusion cloud his consciousness as the other boot catches him in the ribs, forcing the breath from his lungs. He curls into a protective ball. Then he hears Maggie scream.

She shouts at Brendan. 'Stop! Leave him you fucking bastard. You'll kill him.'

His brave, fearless Maggie; his stomach constricts in an onrush of fear. He hears Taylor say, 'that's enough mate.'

Brendan grunts, and Joe tenses for the next onslaught, but it doesn't come. He opens his eyes and waits for the pain to abate, waiting for his vision to clear, trying to get past the searing agony.

Taylor rights Julian in his chair and once upright, Julian shouts. 'You nearly killed me you idiot.'

'Shut up, Julian.' Maggie's voice is icy. 'No one's interested in your whining.'

Joe feels her hand on his cheek and hears her crying.

She turns to Brendan. 'You brute, look what you've done. Joe, Joe, can you hear me? You've killed him. You fuck, you evil bastard.'

Joe smiles, he's never heard Maggie swear like that. He tries to move his head so he can see her. She's a bit blurry, and he coughs. 'I love you my Maggie'.

'Oh Joe,' Maggie strokes hair back from his face. The gesture is so comforting. It reminds Joe of his mother soothing him to sleep as a child, and he wants to nestle into the hand.

'Okay, enough of this Romeo and Juliet bullshit. Maggie, leave him. He's all right. Get up here and find me that rope. No more of these heroics you understand?' Taylor kicks Joe's feet. 'I won't stop Brendan next time. You don't want to leave Maggie bereft do you, although she would make a merry little widow?'

Taylor, all business now, prods Maggie towards the garage to find the rope. Maggie walks obediently along the hallway, but she's thinking of Joe. He tried to save her. He loves her. He stood up to these thugs for her. Why did she think he didn't? He tried to defend her, nothing else matters.

Her panic evaporates. Realising her worst fears has made her forget dread, and anxiety. She'll get the better of these bastards. They think they can come into her house and treat her and Joe like this. She'll make them pay.

Her mind clears, and resolution returns. A plan that's what they need. Joe will have one. She can't let them tie her up, she needs her hands free or she'll be helpless. 'Instead of using rope, why don't you lock us in the walk-in wardrobe in the bedroom? It's big enough and we won't be able to escape. There are no windows. Then you don't have to tie us up and watch us all the time.'

Taylor looks at her sceptically. 'You don't say. And why are you being so helpful suddenly? Where's that rope?'

She points to a cupboard along the nearest wall of the garage. He holds her arm as he opens the cupboard door. Stashed along with wire, twine and other useful gardening things is a coil of rope. It gleams waxy in the diffused light that struggles through yellowing Perspex windows in the panel doors. There is also a role of electrical tape for fencing cattle. Taylor feels the thick cords of towing rope, discarding it in favour of the electrical fencing tape, testing its strength and flexibility.

'I think this one will be easier to tie you up nice and tight.' He turns to Maggie, 'like a trussed pullet. What d'ya think?'

Maggie ignores his jibe and keeps her face frozen. She has another idea, but she can't be tied to the chair. 'What do you want for lunch? The big freezer's over there. She points across the garage. I may as well get something out while we're here, unless you don't want lunch?'

She walks past Joe's car to the freezer.

Taylor's eyes follow her, trying to decide if it's a practical suggestion or if she's planning something devious. 'Yeah, whatever...'

'Do you and Brendan like curry? I make good curry, lamb or chicken?'

'That'll be good.' Taylor looks at her strangely. 'Lamb I think.'

'Lamb takes longer to cook, but we have plenty of time, unless you are in a hurry to get going?'

His gaze is sceptical. 'What do you know? You're up to something, I can tell? Are more people coming?'

'No.'

Maggie buries her head in the chest freezer so he can't see her face. Where are the twins? Why didn't they arrive with Joe instead of those women? Perhaps they escaped. Hope flares. Even now, they'll be calling the police from their mobile phones at the top of the road, but who are the women? She pushes the thought aside.

She needs to focus on practical things. Her head is still fuzzy from the drug. That arsehole, she mutters thinking of Julian's duplicity. Perhaps, if she can get the drugs into the criminals, they might be easier to overcome or at least distracted, until the twins bring the police.

There are lots of them now, but she needs Brendan to put down the pistol. If they're dopey from the drugs, she might seize it, and then... She might get them all killed. What if it goes off killing Joe? No, she won't think about what-if scenarios.

If she makes a curry, she can slip the drugs in without worrying they will taste anything, especially if she puts in lots of chilli. Somehow, she will warn the others not to eat it. All very well, but what if... No, she's not doing what-if's any more, what if nothing. She will do it one step at a time and look for opportunity as she goes.

As she bends over the freezer it dawns on her she is next to Joe's car. What's it doing here? He came in from the terrace. She would have heard him driving into the garage. The door makes a loud grating noise. His car should be on the driveway, or they would have heard him. That German woman said they gave Joe a lift. What's happened? How did Joe get the car back in here and then get a lift?

'What's the hold-up?' Taylor leans in next to Maggie, looking into the freezer. Maggie grabs a chicken.

'Here we are, I can't see any lamb, must be all out. A chicken will have to do.'

She stands up and Taylor lowers the lid of the freezer. He's looking at her strangely again. She squints against the yellow glare that slants through the Perspex. The light casts a pale sickly hue across her face. He knows she's up to something, but he can't figure out what. She's a funny little piece, screwing around behind her husband's back with that long slab of Yankee crap and then acting as though she loves her husband beyond fear. He can see now that the slimy Yankee shit's half her age.

Her skin looks greyish in the yellow light. She's not as young as she appeared last night. Never mind the lamb in the freezer, here's mutton dressed as lamb in her skimpy shorts, and inside out tee-shirt that shows off her nipples. She's got no underpants on either.

Taylor saw her pouty little crack pushing against the crotch of her shorts last night. It was so tempting, but he had to wait until Brendan slept before he could stroke that tightly encased furry little mound. If only Brendan had let him tie her up lying on the floor as he wanted. He could have had her while she was in her drug-induced coma, but he couldn't do much while she was trussed in the chair, not without Brendan knowing.

Just as well now. She'd fooled him into thinking she was a young thing, the fucking hag. She'll pay. Her wide eyes looking up at him are black with smudged mascara and show the crow's-feet. He looks away remembering the dimpled thighs as she had leaned over the freezer and the loosening skin on her upper arms. Taylor doesn't like to be reminded of sagging flesh. He shudders at the memory of his aging mother's puckered mouth coming towards him.

He wants youth and beauty. Old flesh revolts him and now in the light he sees how she tricked him: the fucking old scrubber. He's angry and horny. What he needs is someone young to take his mind off things. The blonde German girl, now that one is more to his taste. No sagging flesh on that piece, just fresh juice. He smiles at the thought.

Taylor's demeanour changes, no longer trying to grope her, and she's relieved, but the look of distaste that flashes across his features frightens her. She feels resolve slipping. How's she going to get the drugs into the curry? He never takes his eyes off her.

'Move.' He points to the door back into the house. Maggie walks in front of him towards the kitchen, but he grabs her shoulder, digging his fingers into her flesh. 'No, lounge room.'

'I have to put the chicken in the microwave to thaw.'

'Lounge!'

Maggie shrugs and continues along the hallway. A flash of inspiration makes her think she must act while he has little room to move. If she can knock him out, she can run for help before Brendan knows what has happened.

She takes a breath and swings around, the frozen bird travelling fast with the momentum, coming up to crash against his skull. Taylor's reflexes are too quick. He blocks her with his right arm, and drops the electrical tape as he grabs her wrist, twisting her arm until she cries out, and drops the chicken.

'You're a bad girl now aren't you Maggie.' His breathing is heavy. 'You need to be punished.'

He pushes her hard against the wall, kicking the roll of electric tape out of his way, and shifts his hand to her throat, pinning her against the wall. It cuts off her air, and with eyes wide with terror, she realises he means to kill her. Her fingers scrabble at his wrist, but his grip is a vice, and her vision darkens.

He watches her struggling to breathe, but he doesn't want her unconscious, just terrified. At the moment before she loses consciousness, he releases the pressure. Then with careful deliberation, he backhands her across the mouth. Maggie's head bangs against the wall, jarring her skull, snapping her neck on her shoulders. He hits her again. Her head jerks back the other way.

The shock is greater than anything Maggie has ever felt before in her life. It isn't pain, not yet. Her ears ring, her vision flashes into paisley patterns with darting and wriggling light worms. Then the pain explodes in her head. She screams and falls in a terrified huddle on the floor.

He kicks her. 'Get up bitch.'

Maggie hears Joe shouting her name then Brendan barks. She scrabbles to her feet. She wants to reach Joe before he does something crazy and they kill him.

'Pick up the chook.' Taylor's booted foot pushes hard against her bottom.

Maggie flies forward to sprawl across the hallway floor. She pulls in her legs and looks back towards Taylor.

He stares, hands on his hips with the same look of disgust as he had in the garage. 'Pick up the chook bitch.' This time he waits for her to stand.

She scrambles to pick it up and stand upright before he hits or kicks her again. Her ears ring, one cheek throbs while the other feels numb, the skin stretching tight over the cheekbone. She tastes metallic ooze from her split lip, and her nose runs with blood or snot, she doesn't know which.

As she limps into the sitting room, Joe sucks in a breath. Fury races through his veins, and his pulse thumps in his temple. He tries to stand up, but Brendan chops the side of his neck again. His knees buckle as his sight dims. He struggles to maintain consciousness, fighting the closing darkness.

Maggie holds the frozen chicken in her finger tips, her head bowed, her hair falling across her face. Blood drips from her nose onto the frozen chicken in small single plops. Taylor prods her towards the sofa with the other women.

Brendan points the pistol at her while Taylor unrolls the electrical tape to tie Joe to the chair. Joe struggles. 'You fucking shithead, look what you've done, can't you see she needs help.'

Taylor's fist catches him full in the face. His nose explodes with pain as he slumps back stunned and disoriented.

Julian watches Joe's struggle, saying nothing, dazed and avoiding confrontation as blood wells from the gash in his forehead where Brendan's belt buckle caught him as he fell. His eyes close and he thinks, 'idiot, he'll get us all killed with his heroics, the fool.'

Tatjana hides her face in Brigitte's shoulder as if not witnessing the action will protect her from its violence. Brigitte pats her shoulder, looking on with hyper-vigilance as her eyes flick around the room searching for something that might help them escape. Neither of them makes a sound.

Brendan drags forward three more chairs from the dining table, and Taylor yanks Brigitte from Tatjana, ordering her to sit. Brigitte resists, and Taylor slaps her across her face. She whimpers and obeys, looking into Tatjana's eyes while Taylor ties her to the chair. Then it's Tatjana's turn. Taylor pulls her up, drawing her into his chest, stroking her hair, running his hands down her back, and around her breast.

Tears well and squeeze from closed eyes to roll down her cheeks.

'Leave the hoor,' Brendan barks.

Taylor manoeuvres Tatjana onto a chair. The beating he gave Maggie aroused him. As he winds the tape around Tatjana, he runs his hands over her body, down the front of her shirt, and around her neck under her hair.

Julian's head comes up, and he watches in fascination. Joe feels sick. He's brought these girls to this danger. It's his fault. He's no better than the arsehole tying up Tatjana. Why did he listen to Maggie? They could have been in Magnetic Island, and Julian would have been here alone when this pond scum arrived. Joe doesn't care what happens to Julian. Look at the filthy slime bag, salivating over Tatjana—so much for Maggie's theory that Julian is gay.

Taylor sees Julian watching, notices his mesmerised excitement, and slides his hands inside Tatjana's shirt and over her breasts, watching as Julian's tongue comes out to run around his lips.

His arousal takes Julian by surprise. Saliva dries in his mouth, his lips parch, and his palms sweat as he watches Taylor undoing Tatjana's buttons. He knows Taylor is playing for his benefit, but he can't help himself.

Joe averts his eyes. He can't help Tatjana either.

'Enough!' Brendan walks in front of Taylor. 'Finish tying them up and stop maggotin' about.'

Once more, Taylor runs his hands over Tatjana's breasts before pulling her shirt closed and tying her to the chair. She'll keep, but who would have thought shit-faced Yankee boy would be such a perve.

'This one next.' Brendan points the pistol at Maggie.

'The slag's going to cook lunch, chicken curry!' Taylor says.

Brendan looks surprised, and then nods. Maggie keeps her head lowered as her body fills with vengeful fury.

14.

Lust

Nausea returns as Julian watches the snivelling German girls. For a moment, he was distracted from his own discomfort by Taylor playing with Tatjana, and he's taken aback at how excited he became given his own circumstances. It was her helplessness against Taylor's power; the lamb of sacrifice. Christ, forget crummy seduction.

He breathes shallowly, trying to avoid his own body odour, the smell of fear dried in his sweat. His arms hurt where the rope cuts into them. Pressure builds in his bowel, and he clinches his sphincter. The lump on his forehead smarts, where something hit him as his chair went over, in that crazy lunge Dr. Williams launched at Brendan. The back of his head throbs too, where he hit it as he crashed to the floor. The fool will get us all killed. He's a bloody university lecturer not a superhero. Whatever possessed him?

Julian remembers his panic of the previous night. He was in a high state of anxiety, as he struggled to pull on his pants, and button his shirt. He tripped and cracked his knee as he ran down the hallway, desperate to avoid Joe catching him in his wife's bed. Being caught sleeping with a lecturer's wife wouldn't augur well for his academic record even if Joe isn't his supervisor. You can never tell who talks to whom and what favours they might want.

When the stranger stepped out of the laundry, confronting him with a raised pistol, he found the scene difficult to comprehend. Not even the menace of a pistol could out-do the relief he felt at it being someone other than Dr. Williams. When they walked into the sitting room and saw Maggie with the other man, his fear turned to anger at the silly bitch.

Maggie was off her face, more so than he expected. She actually flirted with the man called Taylor. What a slut. God, to think he had gone to so much trouble when she would open her legs for anyone.

Last night, he watched Taylor salivating over her. Well he could have her. She was no longer interesting although he found himself surprised at his excitement as he watched through semi-closed eyelashes as Taylor rubbed his hand across Maggie's crotch.

She was in a drug induced sleep and didn't stir. It was her absolute helplessness that excited him, like Tatjana a moment ago, but Maggie hadn't been aware of the activity. Tatjana was acutely aware and terrified. That was infinity more erotic.

Maggie, before she passed out last night, had babbled complete nonsense, asking Taylor and Brendan what their star signs were, for God's sake. She even tried to summon spirits in séance, calling on Taylor to untie her hands. When he refused, she apologised to the spirits for Taylor's ignorance, hoping they would understand.

Julian shudders; he was revolted. What did he see in her? She really is an air head. She carried on like that until Julian wanted to scream at her to shut up. He didn't understand why Brendan and Taylor tolerated the inane chatter. Although he knew the babbling was motivated by ecstasy, the subject matter wasn't; stupid bitch.

At least they don't seem like they're killers. If they were, Brendan would have knocked Maggie off for prattling the way she had. Just as well she passed out. Julian also dozed for a while as Brendan snored.

It was a strange snore with a loud inrush of air ending in a small pheff of exhaled breath. It's what woke him, and that's when he saw Taylor playing with Maggie. He noted that Taylor hadn't done it while Brendan was awake. So, he must be afraid of

Brendan.

Brendan looks bad tempered and anxious all the time whereas Taylor is laid back and cynical, and yet Taylor acquiesces. It's odd, and he wonders how he can use it to his advantage.

His mind flits to Maggie's accusation about the drugs. How did she know? Who told her? Perhaps she isn't as innocent as she pretends. Maybe her ardour last night hadn't just been the MDMA. Perhaps she used it as an excuse. Julian feels uncomfortable about that. He doesn't like being used; manipulating bitch.

The ropes pinch his skin, but trying to wriggle out of them makes it worse, cutting off circulation. The bastards just need to do their thing, whatever that is, and get out of there. They can't hold them forever. Can he sue the Williams for his current danger? Perhaps he'll claim deprivation of liberty, terror, psychological torture while carrying out domestic duties, or some such thing. He'll ask his father's attorneys.

Julian glances at the German backpackers, both silent now. No wonder Joe wasn't worried leaving his slag of a wife. He had a better arrangement, and with two tasty looking morsels. Sly bastard, they are more Julian's age than Joe's.

The dirty old man is as bad as Julian's father, but without the clout of wealth behind him. This seems worse. Playing around for mere sex or love, behind one's spouse's back, is infidelity, but sex for control is the natural course of a man's rights; *droit de seigneur*. For that one needs power, and Dr. Williams is not such a man.

The German women are both attractive in their own way although a bit young for Julian's taste. The dark one looks like a lesbian. She is not someone who would submit easily. The blondie, Tatjana, is more scared and submissive. He is still surprised at how much he was turned on by Taylor's treatment of her. That's power, more so than the thrill he feels seducing compliant women. Having such command over someone as helpless and afraid, is a new turn-on.

He rests his chin on his chest and glances surreptitiously around the room. It's not comfortable, but it is a survival strategy. So long as no one thinks him a likely threat, he'll be left alone, if that idiot Dr. Williams doesn't knock him over with more dumb heroics.

Across the room, Taylor and Brendan talk for a minute before Brendan heads back to the desk and turns on a small transistor radio. Taylor walks back to Maggie. Julian sees the look of disgust crossing his face as he stands over her.

She looks her age this morning with her blacken eyes and swollen cheek. The split lip doesn't help. He hopes Taylor hurt her. The bitch was unnecessarily rough this morning, forking food into his mouth. It made him feel helpless and vulnerable and that makes him angry.

Taylor orders Maggie off the couch and prods her in the back, pushing her towards the kitchen to make lunch. Why does the silly bimbo want to make these two a curry? He glances over at Joe. Stupid bastard is trying to work his hands free.

15.

Despondency

Joe watches Taylor push Maggie out the room. A raging need for revenge surges in his throat. At this moment he understands how easy it would be to kill another human. He struggles with his ropes, but they tighten. He feels powerless. How can he free himself, overpower the men and get Maggie and the two German women out of there before the others arrive? He can't imagine what the bastard will do to his little Abby or his mother-in-law.

Brendan sits at the desk listening to the radio. It's turned down low, and Joe can barely hear what the voice is saying although he catches snatches of a well-known jingle. It's the local station. Joe tries to move his hands to his pocket. If he can get to his Swiss Army knife while Brendan is engrossed, the bastard will pay.

Julian watches Brendan. Useless prick, why hadn't he defended Maggie? Joe flaps his foot to attract his attention, but Julian slides his gaze away, keeping his chin clamped to his chest. Coward. The only time he looked up was when Taylor violated poor Tatjana, and then the perverted bastard was almost drooling.

Shame washes over Joe as he realises he's not much better. He let Maggie down through his own self-pity and selfishness, fooling around with two young women makes him not much better than Taylor. If only he hadn't gone to the waterfall. He should have been here with his wife, especially after she told him she was scared. Joe protests his own accusation; it was a premonition for Christ's sake! They don't exist.

He shakes his head. Never mind. He should have been there for her, and he wasn't. He always fails her when she needs him. Whether premonitions exist or not, Maggie was scared yesterday morning, the same way she was afraid before that bank robbery.

He had dismissed her fears all those years ago, and he had done the same thing again. Waves of remorse sap his determination.

Brigitte sees Joe slump in his chair. She waggles her foot at him. He looks up and she mouths, 'you okay?' He nods and glances at Tatjana who sits in catatonic terror. Tears swell in her eyes and spill unchecked down her cheeks.

He'll have to do something. These women don't deserve this. 'I have a knife,' he mouths.

Brigitte screws her face at him, and he says it again more slowly. She straightens and glances at Brendan. 'What will you do?' Her voice is a low whisper, but it's enough to alert Brendan.

'Shud-up, no talking!' Brendan scrapes his chair across the floor as he gets up and walks over to his captives. He examines their ties before walking out onto the terrace.

Joe can hear the faint sound of the news refrain introducing the mid-day broadcast. Brendan returns. The smell of frying onions, ginger, garlic and chilli waft into the sitting room.

'Turn up the radio,' Joe says. 'I can't hear it over here.'

Surprisingly the man obliges. The news reader says '…the report supports the suspicions that Arafat was killed by rivals of Palestine or Israeli agents. Israel has repeatedly denied any involvement with Arafat's death.' The next item is about the prison escapees.

'Two escapees from Lotus Glen Prison, outside of Mareeba, are still at large and the police are appealing to anyone with information on their whereabouts to contact triple zero or Crime Stoppers. The men are considered dangerous and are alleged to be part of a prohibited criminal motorcycle gang.'

Joe remembers hearing the news item when he ate his breakfast yesterday. It's the same men. How the hell had they found their way here. 'Jesus, that's you!' He stares at Brendan.

'Shud-it.' Brendan bends his head closer to the radio.

'The men have been at large since Tuesday morning after

absconding from the Cairns Court House where they were taken for a hearing relating to alleged arms trafficking charges. They are from New South Wales and are expected to try to make their way back to Sydney. Police have set up roadblocks on all roads out of North Queensland...'

Brendan stands up and walks to the sliding door way to stare out into the garden. His thumb taps the pistol grip as he rocks from heel to toe.

The voice on the radio continues, '...patient as vehicles are stopped and searched. The wanted men are Brendan O'Riley and Taylor Blunt. They are Caucasian, aged forty-five and thirty-nine respectively. O'Riley has an Irish accent. He is approximately 172 centimetres tall, weighs approximately 80 kilos and is described as being of stocky build. He has light blue-grey eyes and receding grey hair, cropped close to his head. He has multiple tattoos on his arms and body. Blunt is approximately 186 centimetres tall and weighs approximately 78 kilos. He is tall, of slim build and has dark brown to black hair and brown eyes. The two men are believed to be travelling in a stolen white Ute, registration number BDZ 849. The men are armed and dangerous and should not be approached...

'Bullshit!' Brendan swings back to the radio and turns it off, then glares at Joe before sitting at the desk and picking up the phone.

He holds the receiver so his hand cups both his mouth and the mouthpiece. Under the desk, his knee jiggles, bouncing the hand that clutches the pistol. His knuckles show as white welts through wiry black hair.

This isn't good. Too much anxiety will make the man erratic. Joe has seen how Brendan behaves when confronted. He renews his efforts to wriggle his hands free. How is he going to overcome

Brendan and get the gun off him?

Brendan, while shorter than Joe, is heavier. The last time Joe had a fight was in grade three. To Brendan, fighting is like breathing, a daily necessity for existence. Joe needs Brendan and Taylor separated if he is to have any hope at all. Will Julian help? Unlikely—it will be down to him and the women.

Joe tries once more to attract Julian's attention with his foot, but to no avail. Joe hisses and Julian flashes him a glance.

'I have a knife. We need to get the pistol.'

Julian shakes his head.

'What d'you mean no!' Joe is astonished.

'Too dangerous,' Julian whispers back.

Brendan turns from his phone call, his fingers clamping over the mouthpiece. 'No talking.'

Julian drops his chin and closes his eyes.

Joe looks at him in disbelief. 'Wanker,' he hisses.

Brigitte signals Joe with her foot. 'I will help. Tell me what to do.'

Joe shakes his head. He hasn't figured that part out yet. 'I don't know. I'm trying to think of something. We have to get the pistol.'

'Excuse?' Brigitte screws her face up at him.

'What?'

'I don't understand.'

'We have to get the gun!'

'Ah, Okay.' Brigitte's face lightens. 'How?'

Joe sighs. The whole thing is impossible, and his bonds are not loosening with all the wriggling. He tries twisting in his chair to see if he can move his hands into his pocket. It's worse. His wrists are raw, and the tape cuts into his upper arms. He won't free himself this way. He'll have to think of something else. Frustrated, impotent and unable to think of a plan, Joe stares at his shoes trying to work out a way of freeing himself and saving his wife and the tourists.

Julian can save himself, the tosser, Joe thinks venomously. His fruitless searching for a clever idea turns to fantasy. He imagines himself saving Maggie, saving the German women, holding the criminals at gunpoint as the police run into the house to make the arrest. The news headlines will say: *Local lecturer's heroic actions capture criminal convicts, saving five lives.*

Julian will cower in a corner while the police arrest the criminals. The newspapers will ask what role the American student played in the rescue, and magnanimously Joe will look the other way with tight-lipped discretion.

Reality intrudes. How can he get from trussed captive to free hero in command of the pistol? If he can't free himself, how will he save anyone? His heroic dreams turn to self-castigation. He's letting Maggie down yet again, making a mess of things. Julian is a coward, but he's a failure. Nothing he set out to achieve in life materialised. No wonder Maggie turns away from him in bed.

It's his fault the German women walked into this trap and ruined their holiday; perhaps even their lives. These kinds of hostage situations can have long-term psychological ramifications for some people. He read about it years ago, wondering if Maggie would develop post-traumatic stress after the bank robbery.

She said she was okay and never mentioned the robbery again. He thought she was resilient, getting over the trauma quickly, putting it behind her. She didn't want to talk about it and when he insisted she cried and shouted at him.

Once he learned to keep his mouth shut, she was fine. That was when she got homesick, and insisted they move north, so she could be closer to her Mum and Dad. She wanted to be as far away from city life as she could get.

North Queensland was Maggie's home not Joe's. He grew up

in Melbourne. Both of his parents died years ago. First his father from a massive heart attack and his mother followed six months later. Some said it was grief, but Joe knows it was a stroke. It all happened less than a year after the bank robbery, and his Dad's legacy enabled them to buy the farm up here.

That legacy still bothers him. After the funeral, sitting listening to the reading of the Will, Joe heard the solicitor talk about Max's share portfolio, property, and the cash at bank as if he was talking about someone other than his morose, but self-effacing father.

Afterwards he asked his Mum if she knew about her husband's wealth, but she just looked at him, pink-eyed with grief and said, 'what wealth dear?'

It was a mystery Joe didn't want to delve into, afraid of what he might find. He could believe anything of his father. Public servants didn't earn that kind of money unless they were corrupt, but he couldn't believe his mother would tolerate it.

There was no evidence of money growing up. Max's job in the public service brought in a comfortable income, but they were never wealthy, or not in a way anyone would notice. After a particularly bad day, when his father nitpicked constantly, his mum said he should mind Dad because he was a good man who came back from Vietnam, a changed man. He harboured resentment and a special dislike for politicians, big business, and any other aspect of the establishment.

Joe had nodded, humouring his mother but deep down he thought his father was a selfish prick who treated him like an imbecile and his mother like a servant. There was no love lost on either side although his mum loved Max, and Joe loved his mum.

Brigitte watches Joe, slumped in his chair with the glazed look of a man distracted by his own inner struggle. What is his plan? Does he have one? If he's got a knife he can cut his bonds, then what?

Despite her frantic foot waggling she can't attract his attention. He's a strange one, screwing both of them yesterday, and then carrying on as if he loves his wife. He certainly didn't want the Ehefrauchen to find out about them. All the elaborate lies he dreamed-up were pathetic in her eyes, but now they are in this mess together. Brigitte feels sorry for him despite everything. She can't blame him for their problems, although she'd like to, but she's realistic enough to know this is one of life's freak coincidences.

She believes in coincidence in a weird way. It's the random nature of it that makes it real. Real life always seems arbitrary and chaotic to her, driven by chance to be either lucky or unlucky. Usually it comes by way of a kick in the guts. Bad luck always seems to loom large, and yet when good luck strikes she often seems to miss the moment. It's only in hindsight, she sees it, and then it all seems so fleeting, yet the bad stuff goes on forever. Tatjana calls her a pessimist, but Brigitte knows it's just reality.

The other man, Julian, is looking at her from under his downcast lashes. He doesn't like her she can tell by the way his glance brushed over her in a kind of sneer. He wants Tatjana. Brigitte doesn't trust him. He looks like a mistkerl—a rotten person, maybe a pervert. Even if he is one of the hostages, she feels no common bond with him.

She glances at Tatjana who has her eyes closed. Poor thing is in shock, paras schieben. She can't blame her, poor madchen. This trip is altogether outside her experience. Brigitte feels to blame. What a mess.

When she met Tatjana at a backpacker's in Darwin, she encouraged the naïve catholic girl to take a risk, and travel around Australia with her, swore to keep her safe on the trip. Tatjana isn't tough like Brigitte. She's led a cloistered life, whereas Brigitte grew up rough. At the time she had an ulterior motive because two people made the trip more affordable, but Tatjana even changed her flight date so they can fly home together at Christmas. Brigitte is responsible whether she likes it or not.

Yesterday she persuaded Tatjana to go along with her because she fancied Joe. Pity he's married although look what he's led them both into— Es ist alles im arsch—It's fucked. How is she going to extract them from this mess? She couldn't care less about the rest of them. They can fry in hell for all she cares, but Tatjana, she has to look after her, she promised.

She looks at her friend's face, shocked by the dark orbs around her pale eyes, like bruised underscores. Tatjana's mouth twitches at the corner, a microscopic movement from which Brigitte takes heart. She smiles back relieved. Tatjana's lips twitch again, and she looks away.

She knows Brigitte is trying to reassure her, and is grateful, but knows she's on her own. No one can help her if that man wants to rape her. The only thing holding him back is the man with the pistol. She needs to get it, but she doesn't know how. They are all tied up except Joe's wife, Maggie.

If only they had never met the son. She can't even remember his name, just a young boy, but like a puppy so eager. His father is better, although a bit old for Tatjana's taste, but Brigitte fancied him. She hadn't minded although she had been so stoned she could barely remember what they did.

Now Tatjana wonders if she will be raped. She imagines it will be bad. She had a foretaste of how bad when that man unbuttoned her blouse while the arschgeige salivated. Da geht mir der arsch auf grundeis. How is she going to get out of this mess? She's scared, but it's her own fault. If only she hadn't insisted on seeing the verdammt frog, but she was obsessed since seeing the piece in the paper. It was so easy to seduce the boy in Townsville to get the information.

Until she'd met Brigitte, Tatjana had never enjoyed such freedom. Now she just wants to go home. An image of her mother's disapproval makes her wince. Her father will be more sympathetic. When she was little her father read her stories, pointing once to a picture of Frigg, and laughing. Tatjana saw the likeness immediately, and whenever she thought of her mother, she would think of Frigg

Gott, how will her parents react when they find out? They'll go nuts. It's bad enough that she invited Brigitte home. Her mother will struggle enough having someone like Brigitte as a guest for Christmas, but if they find out about this, they'll never let Tatjana out on her own again. She has to find a way out that won't create international headlines.

16.

Gluttony

The curry is ready, the rice cooked, and Maggie dawdles, taking ingredients from the fridge to make salad. She racks her brains. How will she get Taylor out of the kitchen?

His fingers drill a tattoo on the laminate. 'Skip the salad.'

She pulls off a handful of lettuce leaves. 'I have to make Joe something to eat. He can't eat curry because he has a heart condition.'

Taylor screws his mouth in contemplation, then nods, but doesn't take his eyes off her. Since she began cooking he has inspected every ingredient she put into the curry, taking spice jars from her and sniffing them, reading the labels of every oil bottle and inspecting each herb. It's driving her crazy. She's becoming desperate, with no opportunity to take the pills from her pocket and stir them into the curry. If only she can distract him.

Earlier, she tried to get him to relax by engaging in conversation, but Taylor was uncommunicative. Gone is the suggestive innuendo and lechery. Gone is his smiling consideration and tenderness. He's a different creature, dour and unpleasant. Maggie wonders if he has one of those psychological problems, something weird like the woman in the drama on the telly, with multiple personalities. She wonders if that makes him more dangerous.

She knows very little about mental illness except what the doctor told her when he referred her to counselling. He blamed the empty nest syndrome, but she knew it wasn't. Oh, it was anxiety all right just the cause wasn't what he said. The stupid pills didn't help either, made her feel sick. Trish was the only one who helped her.

She showed her how to control her environment, and the safety of her family with forecasting and spells. For a while it helped, but in the end, it didn't work either. Look at the trouble she has created by sending Joe to fetch the twins and bring them home. If only she had gone with him to Townsville. How could she have got it so wrong?

It's just lucky the kids must have escaped when Joe was caught. She still can't figure out who the two German women are or what they are doing with Joe. Perhaps she misunderstood, and he gave them a lift although it doesn't explain why his car is in the garage. Never mind, there's no time to think of that, she has to concentrate on getting the drugs into the food.

Resolutely, she tucks her hair behind her ears. She made the mess, now it's up to her to fix it before Taylor or Brendan decides they can't leave witnesses. Taylor doesn't look mentally ill, but he must be, or how else can she account for the sudden change in him? Brendan is even scarier.

Perhaps it's as simple as Taylor transferring his affections to a younger prettier model. Men do that don't they? Maybe he's not mad, just fickle. Oh no, is that why those women are with Joe? Taylor called them Joe's harem. Oh God, Joe's having an affair, and I don't blame him. I've been awful.

Taylor interrupts her self-flagellating thoughts. 'How long does it take to cook this bloody curry?'

'Oh, not long now.' Maggie tosses the salad once more.

The curry has simmered far longer than necessary. It will be stringy, but this isn't a cooking competition. She wants to poison the bastards, not please them, particularly Taylor. The arsehole will suffer in hell for what he's done. She feels her cheek with her finger tips. The swelling stretches her skin tight. One eye is puffy and half closed.

Earlier she caught her reflection in the steel pot base. Maggie never thought of herself as vain, but now she'll be scarred and ugly for life. Joe will be disgusted, not only by her betrayal, and abandonment to Julian, but because she'll look hideous, a constant reminder to him of her adultery.

She shies away from the word, but that's what it is, and she's determined to face the consequences so long as they don't include losing Joe. She loves him and doesn't know what possessed her these past few months. Her stomach fluttered when she met with Belinda's father, and she lied about Julian being gay, but she didn't intend any of it to go further.

All she wanted was to feel special, loved and admired, now all she feels is shame. She's despicable and ugly, and can't even do a simple thing like slip a few drugs into the curry. Only the criminals must eat it, although she doesn't really care if Julian or one of the women does, especially if it's the one having an affair with her husband. She'll be happy to feed her the drugs, personally, and give Julian an overdose. The in-grown arsehole has it coming after last night, but unless the women are guilty as charged, they don't deserve it, whoever they are.

How did they get here? Why is Joe's car in the garage when she didn't hear the panel door opening? She shakes her head. If only she could distract Taylor. She leans over the pot to taste the curry and an idea forms.

'Taylor, come over and taste this. What do you think it needs—salt perhaps?'

Taylor hesitates, then walks over and slurps at the spoon of sauce she holds out. His face relaxes in surprise, and he takes the spoon from her, licking the buttery yellow sauce from it with relish.

'Tastes good; needs nothing, you're a good cook.'

'I know what, it probably needs coriander. It's growing in the garden. Please can we get it? It'll make it taste so much better.'

'Where abouts?' Taylor is suspicious, but the curry is bloody lovely. She wasn't lying.

'Just around the corner of the house.' Maggie points, 'you can watch me while I get it. You won't regret it.'

'Okay, but no tricks or I'll have to punish you again.' Taylor grins. He enjoys her fear, and he wouldn't mind the opportunity to hit her again. He might do it anyway before he has Tatjana. Distracted by his arousal, he realises Maggie has walked across the kitchen and is opening a drawer.

'What're you doing?'

'Getting scissors.'

'Oh no you don't. I'll take those.' Taylor takes them from her and gestures for her to lead the way.

Outside, in the herb garden, he bends to cut the coriander, and she plunges her hand into her pocket, palming the packet before he looks back at her. He straightens with a small bunch of herb clutched in his grasp.

'More,' she says, 'cut more.'

He bends again to cut more of the herb, and then straightens saying, 'enough.'

It is enough. Maggie has the pills tucked into the base of her clamped fingers, and the packet is back in her pocket. She takes both bunches of herb from him, and he doesn't notice her crabbed fingers.

She skips back to the kitchen with Taylor striding behind her and stuffs the coriander leaves into the food processor, releasing the pills from between her fingers, then sprinkles in salt, hoping to disguise any white powder in the mix. As an afterthought, she adds a small spoonful of sugar, hoping it will disguise any bitterness. Once the coriander is chopped finely, she stirs it into the curry.

Her heart races as she pushes a laden tea trolley through to the sitting room. All she needs to do now is make sure Brendan and Taylor eat a lot of curry, and that she and Joe eat none. She needs to be alert for an opportunity to get the pistol. Joe can hold it while she calls the police, if the twins haven't already done that.

She hopes they are okay, but what if something has gone wrong? Perhaps, their mobiles are flat or out of credit. It would be typical of Abby, but Paul is more reliable. A flat mobile will mean an eight-kilometre hike before they can get to a public phone. No, surely they would go to the neighbours first. Perhaps the neighbours aren't home. Maggie pushes the intruding thoughts aside; Joe is always telling her she teases imponderables fruitlessly. She will stop.

As she walks into the sitting room Joe makes strange eye signals at her. Her eyebrow goes up in question, but the movement breaks the blood clot and it stings. She brushes the dribble away and feels a rush of tenderness towards her husband. He looks as battered as she feels, and he got his punishment in defence of her. She smiles in reassurance, glancing at Brendan to make sure he's not looking, and mouths, 'don't eat the curry.'

Brendan hangs up the phone and turns to Taylor. 'They'll bring a clean car tonight.'

Taylor nods and glances over to where Maggie has parked the trolley.

Joe hopes they'll be gone by the time Stan and Elaine arrive with the twins. He wants the bastards to escape, not permanently, but just so they leave the house. Then he'll call the police as soon as they have gone. Perhaps the whole thing will blow over by the time the twins arrive, but doubt creeps into his mind.

What if they don't leave? What will they do to the kids? He's seen what they're capable of doing. Will they risk leaving witnesses? It's unlikely. Christ, he has to do something before that.

Joe smells the curry and saliva spurts from his tongue. His stomach clamours for food. He hasn't eaten since lunch yesterday. Surely, they won't let their captives starve. That gives him an idea. When they free his hands to eat, he'll be able to get to his knife, and jump Taylor. Then with a knife held to the bastard's throat, Brendan will be forced to drop the pistol. Maggie can pick it up and then free the others.

Buoyed, he tries to convey reassurance to Maggie. He has a plan and she should follow his lead. She has amazing intuition, and sometimes he swears she can read his mind.

Taylor looms behind her and prevents Joe making any more signs, but it doesn't matter, she will get the gist. What a team they make.

Maggie gives a little frown as she watches the animation crossing Joe's face, and see's him angle sideways, shaking his shoulder at her and grinning like he's on ecstasy. She can't think why he should be so excited although it's better than the somnolent despair in which Julian wallows, slouched in his chair. Embarrassment clogs her throat as she realises it was only yesterday she thought him dashing and romantic. Now, all she sees is a cowardly pimple of humanity.

Brendan hangs up the phone. For a moment Maggie is cranky at the thought of the phone bill. Then it dawns on her, he is a criminal, a gangster and a killer, and the police will be very interested in the numbers he calls.

Brendan frightens her more than Taylor, despite the beating. He looks like a man who will lose control, a brute. At least Taylor is educated, and has an understanding of risk and consequence. After all, he stopped Brendan from killing Joe earlier.

She piles rice and curry onto plates and hands them to the criminals. Then she walks over to sit on the sofa. Brendan sniffs at the curry.

'There's nothing in it mate. I watched her carefully,' Taylor says.

Brendan shakes his head. 'Why has she only dished up two plates then?'

Maggie interjects, 'I didn't know if you would let us eat.'

Brendan turns his long indifferent stare on her. 'Feed them,' he says pointing at Brigitte and Tatjana.

'No. We are vegetarians.' Brigitte speaks urgently.

Joe says, 'untie us so we can eat by ourselves.'

'Shud ye gob.'

Maggie knew from the breakfast ritual, they wouldn't untie anyone. She moves from the sofa to dish up another plate, but instead of going to the women, she walks over to feed Julian.

Brendan suspects Maggie's compliance and snaps, 'feed your husband first.'

Taylor holds out a restraining hand saying, 'he has a heart condition. Let her feed the boyfriend, and we will see if this curry is okay.'

Maggie risks a swipe at them, hoping Joe hasn't noticed the boyfriend bit. 'Oh for God's sakes, what am I running here, a restaurant? Don't eat; what do I care?' She pulls up a chair to sit in front of Julian.

Joe feels a surge of irritation as saliva fills his mouth. What's Maggie doing? Why has she ruined his plan? He doesn't have a heart condition. What does Taylor mean, calling Julian her boyfriend? He tries to catch her eye.

Maggie holds up a fork full of curry, but Julian is suspicious and turns his face away, his mouth pressed shut. Maggie sighs and glances at Taylor.

'Eat dickhead,' Taylor demands, but Julian shakes his head.

Maggie is in a panic now. Julian will give the game away. She stands up, placing the plate on her chair and grabs his head, forcing the fork between his teeth as she hisses, 'eat you treacherous bastard.'

He gags as she stuffs food into his mouth. Taylor is amused by Maggie force feeding Julian, but Brendan remains as sour as usual.

She turns to them. 'You'd better eat up too, or it will get cold.'

Taylor sits at the dining table and scoops food into his mouth. After all, he watched Maggie prepare it, and he was vigilant. Eventually, Brendan plonks himself on the sofa, and shovels large mouthfuls between his lips. He eats quickly, his pistol resting on the cushion beside him.

Joe tries again. 'Untie us so we can eat.'

They ignore him. Maggie finishes feeding Julian and goes back to the trolley. She fills a bowl with salad and walks back to Joe. She mouths, 'curry's drugged.'

'No talking,' Brendan says with his mouth full. 'Good curry this!'

Taylor nods.

Maggie folds lettuce leaves in a parcel and stabs it with a fork. Then she holds it to Joe's mouth.

'I have a knife in my left pocket,' he whispers. Maggie remains stony-faced pushing salad into his mouth, but he knows she's understood.

While Brendan and Taylor are occupied, Joe shifts his body, angling towards her, but the pocket is caught in the crease of his leg, and the opening is too tight.

Brendan sees Maggie's hand drop to her husband's knees and says with his mouth full, 'wad're doing? Leave him. Move away. He's had enough.'

Reluctantly, Maggie moves. Brendan gets up with his plate and fork still in hand and walks over to appraise the captives as he continues shovelling food into his mouth. Eventually, he moves to the trolley where he refills his plate. He didn't realise how hungry he was. This morning's breakfast wasn't enough.

Brendan sits down again to eat. Food always calms him, and he watches Maggie as she sits on the sofa, eyes downcast. She makes a good curry. He'll give her that even though she said she's a witch and speaks to the dead.

He makes the sign of the cross, fork clutched in hand, not sure if she's crazy. Taylor said it was just drugs talking, but he shivers. Worry gnaws at his stomach. Not that he's afraid of much, but witchcraft, magic and the dead are a different matter. What if she's telling the truth?

He shovels the food in faster and looks down with surprise when his plate is empty. Last night, she seemed to know an awful lot about him, calling him by his star sign, telling him he's Capricorn with a Libra Moon and Aries rising. She told Taylor he is Sagittarius, with a Scorpio moon and Leo rising. He doesn't know what it means except she's right about him being Capricorn and Taylor being Sagittarius.

'Lucky guess,' Taylor said calming Brendan's fears, but maybe it wasn't a guess, maybe she is psychic. Brendan's wary, but also curious. This woman could tell him things. Things he wants to know, but things the Nuns cuffed him around the head for asking. He had found no one else to ask. Maybe, if she can talk to the dead, she could talk to his mother.

Brendan crosses himself again. He's not sure he wants to be party to that, even his mother. The Nuns said it was a mortal sin, and he would burn in hell. Not that he believes all that bullshit now, but one never knew, not really. He would like to tell his mother he is sorry. Brendan feels anxiety building. It forces him to his feet, and he goes to fill his plate again. Food will stop the nerves in his stomach.

Maggie watches him scooping down great mouthfuls. He's

deep in thought, and she wonders why as he makes a fisted cross over his left breast for the second time. She glances across to Taylor. He savours his food, methodically picky, almost finicky in the way he separates each forkful of rice before scooping the curry on top of it, and lifting the whole to his mouth.

Brendan has eaten three helpings before Taylor finishes his first. With great relief she watches him refill his plate. She doesn't know how much they need for the drugs to have any effect, but she doesn't care if they both die from an overdose.

17.

Evil

It's mid afternoon, and Brendan's incessant pacing to and fro across the room is driving Taylor nuts. He is sprawled across the sofa picking bits of curry from his teeth. It was delicious, but he ate too much, and now his stomach feels about to burst. He wants a coke to wash it down, but the stupid bitch has none, calls it poison.

'Okay mate?' he asks Brendan, hoping he will stop moving, and sit down on the sofa. Taylor feels queasy and all this pacing is making it worse.

Brendan shakes his head, but continues to pace. The corners of the room have a pinkish haze like mist obscuring the edges. The colours coalesce into spiralling wisps that spread out through the room. He looks around to see if anyone else has noticed.

Sweat runs off Taylor, and he gets up from the sofa to go outside to the terrace for air. Brendan watches him leave and wonders if he should say something about the colours, but it seems daft. Perhaps he's having an episode like that woman he married to get Australian residency. She saw colours when she heard music. Brendan thought she made it up, like it was proof of her clairvoyant ability or something. He was grateful to her for keeping him from having to go back to Ireland, where he was wanted by those cursed Proddies, the so called fooking UVF, so he pretended to believe her. Perhaps it was real after all.

He rubs his eyes and tries to ignore the colour by making himself busy. He checks the ties on the captives' hands. Joe has tried to get his hands free, but instead has tightened the tape around his arms. Fool. He checks Julian. There's something wrong with the bloke. Brendan stands over him and watches. Julian has his head on his chest, but he's grinning as if he alone knows the joke.

Brendan grabs his hair, and yanks his head. 'What you grinning at fool?'

Julian tries to marshal his features, but he feels so good. Even the thug pulling his hair doesn't seem so threatening. He can feel the effects of the MDMA, and knows what Maggie's done. Silly bitch included the acid; colours are intense and time seems to slow.

Maggie's not sure what's happening, but she can see an effect on Julian and Brendan. Taylor looks unaffected, just a little pale. She glances across at Joe, but he's staring at the floor, still trying to work out a plan. He berates himself to ease his impotent rage.

Maggie hopes Julian and Joe don't give the game away before the drugs have a chance to work. She wishes she knew what symptoms to expect. The only experience she's had, other than the tablets the doctor gave her, is what she felt last night. She put all the pills into the curry, and they have eaten most of it, so hopefully it will knock them out.

Brendan checks Tatjana and Brigitte's ties. When he leans over, Brigitte spits at him. He back hands her across her mouth with the hand clutching the pistol. The force flings her back against Tatjana and she slumps in a daze. Her split lip oozes blood, which runs unchecked down her chin.

The action brings Tatjana out of her paralysis as rage filters through her veins. Hatred threatens to overwhelm her with its intensity, and she stares at Brendan with murder in her heart. Brendan turns away oblivious to the change.

Maggie makes herself small and still. They haven't tied her up, and she is hoping Brendan won't notice, but as he walks towards her she fears he will soon see the mistake. Instead, he stands before her, and says, 'what're you up to witch?'

Taylor returns from outside and saves Maggie from having to respond. His olive skin was pale when he went out, but now it has a yellowish tinge like the blanched skin of a boiled almond. He says to Brendan, 'you right to watch them a minute? I need the crapper.'

Brendan nods, and Taylor leaves the room in a hurry. That curry seems to have gone right through him. The bitch must have put something in the food, and it's giving him the squitters although he doesn't know how she did it. He watched everything go in, and even though he didn't know what half the spices were, he could see they were from a supermarket. Maybe he's allergic. He's sweating and nauseous as he hurries down the hallway to the bathroom. She must have done something.

The whore said she was a witch. Witches know potions, don't they? He doesn't believe in all that garbage. It's superstitious crap. His stomach cramps. He's losing control of his bowels. His heart's racing. Christ he's having a heart attack, he can feel it.

He sits on the lavatory seat just in time as with a gush he evacuates his bowel. As he slumps on the seat, nausea rises in his throat and he bends forward feeling like he will vomit. He's losing control of his mind. Christ, get a grip, he berates himself. Then a loud croak reverberates through the room.

In the sitting room, Maggie takes a breath. She has to act while Taylor is out the room. Brendan still stands before her, immobile and staring. She puts tenderness into her low voice as she says, 'Brendan, someone wants to talk to you.'

It takes a moment for Brendan to register what she is saying. He looks around fearfully.

'Bullshit!' but the pink mist coalesces into a form in front of him. He begins to shake. Who's it... Ma?

Maggie is relieved she has struck the right cord. 'Yes Brendan, your Ma's here. She wants to talk to you.'

Joe watches in amazement as Brendan takes two steps away from Maggie. He stands in the middle of the room staring at the standard lamp. Joe can't make out what absorbs him.

'Ma?' Brendan says tentatively, 'Ma, is that you?'

Julian sniggers, and Brendan rounds on him. 'What you laughing at freak?'

Maggie says in her most soporific voice, 'ignore him Brendan. Your Ma wants you to know she loves you.'

Brendan turns back to the lamp. 'She's gone.'

'No, she is still here, but she doesn't like Julian laughing at her. She wants to talk to you. She's been waiting so long...'

Brendan walks over to Julian and presses the pistol muzzle against his forehead. 'Make a sound again freak and I'll kill you— get-it?'

Julian's bowel liquefies and his sphincter relaxes. Brendan has seen fear do that before and with satisfaction he turns away. The unexpected odour drifts into Tatjana's nostrils, wrenching her from focusing on her own trauma.

She glances across to see Julian slump in his chair. His eyes squeeze closed, and his chin clamps to his chest as he takes in sobbing gulps of air. To her amazement she sees he is crying like a little boy. Her disgust deepens.

Brendan is furious at the sobbing noise and the rising smell. He grabs the back of Julian's chair to drag him outside to the terrace. 'Ye filthy disgusting bastard, outside ye go.' Brendan checks his ties and returns inside, leaving Julian on the terrace. As he enters through the sliding doors he sees Maggie standing by Joe's chair. 'What ye doing bitch?'

Maggie pulls herself up straight and scolds, 'Brendan watch your language, your mother's listening.'

Brendan wavers and glances behind him. His mind tells him it isn't possible, but he wants to believe, and he's seen the pink haze.

This is not his imagination. He saw the outline of his mother in her Sunday hat, and felt an immense sense of well-being, of love.

Even though the form was indistinct, he knew it was his mother. Only a mother's love could make a man feel such a thing, but now she's gone. He can't see the pink haze any more either and it's that fooking idiot's fault. The witch has to bring her back or he'll kill the stinking maggot.

Maggie worries she has lost Brendan. He is staring at her again as if in a trance. She daren't move. She needs him to re engaged in whatever he believes is happening.

'Sit down witch. Get away from there.' Brendan waves the pistol at Maggie. The air bends and wavers in the wake of a pink ark left by his moving arm. He watches fascinated. 'Ma, is that you?'

Maggie takes a small step away. Joe holds his breath. That she has a plan is clear, but what's up with Brendan. Is it the drugged curry? Julian is behaving strangely too.

Joe tries to work out what kind of drug Maggie put in the curry. Mentally he goes through the medicine cabinet, but he can't think of anything that could be used to drug them. Perhaps she has some of her anti-depression medicine left although he can't imagine what effect it could have.

He gives up, relieved that Maggie has a plan. He tries to look reassuringly at Tatjana and Brigitte, to convey confidence. Brigitte stares back at him, blood drying on her lip. Her gaze is accusing as if it's his fault, and she's right. Tatjana watches Brendan with focused fury.

Joe turns his head to see what Brendan is doing. Maggie, his brave resourceful Maggie, purrs at the man. How she has the presence of mind, he doesn't know, but his chest fills with pride as he watches her take control of the thug.

'Brendan your mother wants to speak with you.'

'Sit down there, now!' Brendon shouts.

Maggie obeys. She has missed her chance. There wasn't enough time to get the knife from Joe's pocket. Getting Brendan to believe his Ma is here, is all she had left. Brendan picks up the roll of electric tape, and Maggie realises he's going to tie her up, and in desperation, tries again.

She stares past him as if someone loiters in the background. 'Brendan, your Ma says to talk to her, she doesn't have much time.'

Brendan swings back, his eyes wide, showing signs of his drug befuddled mind. 'Where is she? Why doesn't she talk to me?'

'She can't Brendan,' Maggie's voice soothes. 'She can only talk through a Medium. That's why she's talking to me.'

Maggie hopes the spirits forgive her for pretending she's a Medium, but Brendan is ignorant of that.

His voice whines as he challenges Maggie to prove it. 'What's she saying then?' He wants his Ma to talk to him. Can he trust the witch?

'She's not saying anything, but I can see her. She's crying. She wants us to join hands, form a circle. We need to give her the circle of protection. It's like I said last night Brendan, we need the circle so she can cross over to speak with you.' Maggie points to the dining table. 'If we sit there, and join hands she'll be safe, but you must hurry Brendan or you'll lose her forever.' Maggie holds her breath. Has she gone too far?

'You're lying. It's a trick.' Brendan licks his lips, vacillating. What if it's true? If he doesn't act and lets his mother down again, will he get another chance? Witches can do this sort of thing, séances and stuff, he knows that.

'No Brendan, it's not a trick. You saw her. I know you saw her. If you concentrate you'll see her again.'

Brendan crosses himself. He did see her. She is here. The

witch isn't lying because he saw her. His face creases in concentration as he tries to conjure her image again, and he peers into the space where he last saw the pink light. Slowly, a shape begins to form around the lamp in front of him. He's exhilarated, his heart pounds, and his skin feels clammy.

A breeze blows in from the open doors, carrying the fetid stench of Julian's jeans. Brendan knows it's the smell of the grave. He glances towards the doorway; it glows with light spreading out across the room. The hair on his neck prickles, and tears well in his eyes.

'Ma.' He falls to his knees, 'Ma, oh Ma forgive me. Speak to me Ma, please speak to me. Tell me you forgive me. Please Ma.'

'She's calling for the circle Brendan. Please, she hasn't much time. They're drawing her back.'

'Who? Who's drawing her back?'

'The spirit world Brendan; she doesn't have much time, give her the circle so she can speak to you.'

Brendan makes up his mind. He puts down the tape and tells Maggie to go to the table.

'Two people are not enough Brendan,' Maggie says gently. 'We need three at least and five is better. It doesn't work with even numbers.' She says making up the first thing that comes to mind.

Brendan hesitates. 'We'll wait for Taylor. He'll be three.'

'We don't have time Brendan. Your mother's fading.'

Brendan looks around the room and the radiant light has gone; he's going to let his Ma down again. Where the bloody hell is Taylor? He can't free another one, or can he? He has the pistol. He looks at the two German women—the fair one; she's too scared and small to be any threat. 'Untie her,' he says pointing at Tatjana.

Tatjana shrinks back and shakes her head at Maggie.

Maggie leans close, whispering, 'it'll be all right. I'll look after you.'

Brigitte nods, 'do it Tatjana.'

Maggie picks at Tatjana's bonds, but the knots are too tight to undo.

'Hurry up, what's taking so long?' Brendan is impatient now he has decided. He won't lose his mother through the witch's fumbling.

Maggie looks pleadingly at Brendan. 'We'll have to cut the tape. I can't untie it.'

Brendan is afraid he'll lose the opportunity to speak with his Ma, and takes the bread knife from the trolley to slash Tatjana's bonds. Everything seems to move in slow motion.

Tatjana gets up, rubbing her wrists as she walks to the table. He follows her, the pistol aimed at her back. The bread knife is still clutched in his left hand. The light bends and ripples as she moves, and Brendan knows the room is full of magic.

Maggie sits at the table holding Brendan's right wrist as his hand clutches the pistol. Tatjana's arm stretches across the table clutching Brendan's left wrist above the hand with the bread knife. If only she was strong enough to grab it and wrestle it away, but the man is twice her weight.

Maggie looks at the pistol. Can she snatch it away? No. She must use guile or he'll throw her off in a heartbeat, and shoot her before she hits the ground. She squeezes Tatjana's hand. The poor woman looks terrified.

Maggie racks her brains for a plan as she lowers her head, calling for the spirit of Brendan's mother to speak. Outside, in gathering gloom, the sounds of a distant pack of Dingos howling as they hunt their prey, floats up from the valley. Clouds quicken, darkening the late afternoon landscape, as the evening mist rises from the rivers and unfurls across the paddocks. Its clammy breath swirls in through the open doors.

Brendan waits, oblivious to his surroundings, hyper-vigilant and enraptured as he prepares to meet his mother and gain her forgiveness.

Down the hallway in the guest bathroom, Taylor lies on the floor, stiff with terror. The cold tiles waver and shiver like quicksand under his naked buttocks. The floor seems alive as if a beast heaves beneath the tiles. If he falls through, it will swallow him.

The croaking voice calls out again, reverberating around the room. Taylor is too afraid to move in case he dislodges a wavering tile and gets sucked into the vortex. Eventually, he recognises it's no beast, just his father choking with horror as he stands in the doorway watching his wife and son naked on the bed.

Taylor feels hands around his throat and begs for mercy. It's not his fault. Father should have protected him. He isn't a mummy's boy. He hates mummy.

He looks back at his father who kneels over his mother holding her wrist, but it's too late for a pulse. Mummy lies in a pool of blood, her lips loose, red, and flaccid in wrinkled, powdery skin. It's her fault. She had to die.

The distant dingo howls, sound like his father wailing, as they cart him off to prison. He's sorry. 'Please, please...' Taylor calls out, curling into a foetal ball, arms covering his head.

Outside a car door slams, bringing him to his senses. He hauls himself up from the tiles and hobbles to the window, but he can see nothing through the pebbled glass. He turns and stumbles, falling against the shower door. Then he realises his trousers are around his ankles, and bends down, but as he does his vision darkens. It takes a moment to regain balance.

His heart hammers, and sweat runs rivulets down his forehead and flanks. There's another loud croak. This isn't real. He's hallucinating. The bitch put something in their food. His stomach cramps again, and he doubles over the toilet bowl.

The floor gapes sickeningly beneath his feet. It's not real, he tells himself, it's not real. He has to get back to Brendan and warn him.

18.

To Covet and Command

Stan pulls into a car park outside the hotel in Innisfail. Across the road the mighty Johnson River roils through ragged remnants of rainforest towards the sea. Moored boats strain against their ropes to bob alongside a boardwalk.

An heroic canecutter stands on his stone plinth, concentrating on cutting his cane while Indian Myna birds squabble for place on his hat. A dog lifts its leg against the statue's protective railing. Up the hill, away from the river, a majestic white cathedral rises in spire pointing glory, a testament to the devoted Italian Catholics who pioneered this land. In the distance an elaborate Art déco water tower rises above the trees.

'I'll just pick up a six pack or two. Do you want anything?' Stan looks at his wife in the passenger seat.

She shakes her head and then changes her mind, 'perhaps a bottle or two of that nice Sav Blanc we bought last time. Maggie likes that.'

'Do you remember its name?'

Elaine shakes her head again. 'Never mind, just if you see it.'

'I know which one.' Abby unclasps her seat belt. 'I'll come with you Pops.'

Paul needs to stretch his legs. 'Are you staying in the car Gram?'

Elaine nods.

'Do you mind if I go, just to stretch a bit.'

Stan and Abby are already out the car and walking towards the hotel entrance.

Elaine says, 'don't be long dear. It's getting late. I want to be there before dark.'

Paul follows Pops and Abby into the hotel. As he goes inside, he sees Pops talking to a man. Paul joins them, noticing his sister twisting her long hair around her fingers. She's gazing up at the man in breathless adoration. God she is embarrassing.

Stan turns as he arrives. He clasps Paul's shoulder. 'Son, meet a man you might like to talk to about a career in the force. He has an interesting life, and it's not behind a desk. Chris Zonda, my grandson Paul.'

Paul shakes the man's outstretched hand. His grip is firm, his hand enormous, his forearms bronzed and sinewed. Paul feels a little daunted and wonders what can be so interesting about policing that his grandfather hasn't told him stories about, endlessly. 'What do you do?'

Chris grins. 'Catch bad guys mate.'

Paul feels drawn to him. There is something about the bloke, almost as if you have been mates forever.

Stan explains. 'Chris is with the Special Emergency Response Team. They do the stuff that's too tricky and dangerous for the regular police.'

Paul is interested. He's heard about SERT.

Stan says, 'what're you doing in this neck of the woods— chasing the fugitives?'

Chris nods and looks around the room. 'In a way, yeah. We got a call about a situation at a farmstead, but false alarm, or rather a different lot of bad guys, not the escapees. We're just on our way back to Cairns. How long are you here for Stan? I'm off duty tomorrow for a few days. Maybe we can grab a beer if you're free?'

'Sure, I'll be up at my daughter's place. Give me a call.'

'Ah, yes.' He looks towards the door at another bloke gesturing. 'I have to go mate. I'll call you. Nice to meet you Paul, Abby.'

His gaze lingers on Abby's face for a second before he turns to hurry out the door. There's something familiar about her. Ah, he knows what it is. She looks like her mother. He didn't have time to tell Stan he had met his daughter, but he'll catch up with him later.

As he leaves, Abby gazes after him. He's a god. She has to get her Pop to invite him around to the farm. 'Pops, you can invite him for lunch or something.'

Stan ignores her and says, 'go find the wine for your Gram while I get the beer. There's a good girl.'

Twenty minutes later, they drive up the Highway towards the mountains. Paul gazes out the window wondering if policing might be an option after all. That bloke Chris made it look cool. He leans forward, his hand on the back of Pops seat. 'Pops what does it take to get into SERT?'

Abby, reading a book, snorts in derision. 'They only let hunks in, not dweebs.'

Stan casts a dark look in the rear-view mirror, and Abby drops her head pretending to be engrossed in her book, but she's listening.

It's a pretty gruelling training course, mentally and physically, but if you're fit and determined you could do it. Are you still contemplating a career with the police? It's not a bad choice son.'

'I don't know, but it might be interesting.'

'I'll talk to Chris about showing you around if you like, but only on condition you finish Uni first. Plenty of time later, to join up, once you have your degree.'

Stan turns off the main highway and as they near the farm road, Paul gazes out the window at familiar landmarks. A sense of excitement builds as they near the farm. He's glad to be home. 'Hey Abbs look, they've extended the dairy.'

He points to a half built shed adjoining the dairy of a neighbouring farm. Abby hums and glances up, but she isn't interested. She returns to her book. Paul doesn't want to admit it, but he misses home. Misses his mother, misses Dad too, but mostly Mum and home cooked food. Abby never seems to miss home as much, but looking at her now, he senses behind the laconic comments and bored façade, she is just as excited.

He worries about his Mum, and hates it that it's their absence that makes her sad. The Easter break was the worst, but she seemed to be over it when they went home at the end of the first semester. The conversation with his Dad yesterday made Paul worry his Mum is sick again.

He regrets telling Abby about her premonition; she had another hissy, went all indignant and know-it-all. He shouldn't give in to Abby when she hassles him, but it's hard to keep her at bay. It always ends in him telling her stuff, just to shut her up. He hates it when she says things about Mum and Dad. Abby once said she was allowed because they are her parents, but Paul doesn't agree. He knows exactly why his Dad phoned him, not Abby, and he sympathises.

Pops slows to enter the long driveway to the farmhouse. Paul sees a van up ahead and wonders idly who might be visiting. Judging by the battered campervan covered in rude graphics, it's not one of his parents' friends. Perhaps they are Dad's students.

Pop says, 'who have we here?' The question's rhetorical, but Abby pulls herself forward to look over Gram's shoulder. The van is parked in the middle of the drive, blocking their way. Its doors are open, but the van is empty.

'Bloody idiot. Who parks like that?' Pops pulls on the handbrake.

'I'll go and get someone to move it shall I?' Paul has the door open and is half way out of the car, when Pops sees the Ute ahead.

'Hold on Paul, something's wrong here.' Stan feels a prickle of warning run up his neck. It's an instinct he's learned to heed.

On the driveway, beyond the Ute, lies an abandoned backpack. He hasn't been a policeman all his life without reading the signs, knowing when something is wrong.

'Best I come with you…quietly now. Elaine,' he glances at his wife, 'you and Abby stay here.'

She nods.

'I don't like this.' He leans across and takes a set of handcuffs from the glove compartment. 'Better safe than sorry,' he grins at his wife, and opens his door.

Worry flashes across Elaine's face, but she straightens to turn, and give Abby a reassuring smile.

'Why the handcuffs?' Abby looks frightened.

Paul slams the door, and Stan winces. 'What part of quietly now, did you miss boy?'

'Sorry.'

'Quietly now, walk behind me.'

Paul looks at Pops askance. The old man has flipped. 'What is it Pops?'

'Don't know son, but something's wrong. This van, that Ute… see that bag…' he points. 'Something's not right.'

Paul says nothing, but he's thinking, someone dropped a bag, so what.

Pops screws up his eyes. 'Can you make out the number plate?' His large grizzled hand rests on Paul's arm.

Paul looks down at the restraining hand, but humours him. 'Yes it's something DZ 84 something, nine I think. It's hard to tell at this angle, in this light.'

Stan's breath comes out in a rush. It's the vehicle stolen by the fugitives. His antenna for danger hasn't failed. What are they doing here? Good place to hide out, he supposes. What to do? He pulls out his phone. No signal. Of course not! Nothing works out in this God forsaken wilderness.

A smattering of rain lands on his face as the tree branches overhead rip the mist to shreds. The gloom silences the birds, and it begins to rain.

He pulls Paul close and says in a low voice, 'don't question me boy, but I want you to go back to the car, reverse out the driveway as quietly as you can. Don't slam any doors. I want you to drive to the top of the road until you get a mobile signal, then I want you to call the police, triple zero you understand. Tell them, the escaped prisoners are at the farm. They have your Mum and Dad hostage—get it? Hurry now.'

Paul gapes at his grandfather. He's not sure if it's one of Pops silly games or if the old man has really lost it.

'You're serious?'

'Yes son, go do it now. Hurry.'

'How do you know?'

'That's the escaped crims car. I know boy, don't question me or we'll blow it—go now.'

He says it with such urgency and authority that Paul turns to run back to the car. He gets into the driver's seat without a word, hardly closing the door so as not to make a noise. He starts the engine, backing out of the drive as instructed. Elaine looks alarmed, but she sees Stan gesturing to her. He must have given Paul instructions. She pulls her seat belt back around her, and waits for Paul to tell her what is happening.

Abby is not so calm. She sits forward in the backseat asking shrilly, 'What're you doing?' When no one answers, she hits Paul on the shoulder, repeating 'what are you doing?' Fear creeps up Abby's throat, but she doesn't know why. She glances back down the driveway to see Pops in a strange crab-like run.

Paul turns out of the driveway and onto the road before pressing his foot hard on the accelerator. The car leaps forward, wheels spinning in the gravel. It skids sideways before gaining traction and shooting off down the road. Only then does he say anything. 'Gram, tell me when we have a mobile signal. We have to call triple zero. Pops says Mum and Dad are hostages.'

Abby shrieks, 'Paul, what's happening?'

'Shut up Abby,' Elaine opens her handbag to find her mobile phone. 'Go on Paul?'

'Pops says it's the escaped criminals. He recognised the Ute number plate up near the house.'

Paul focuses on keeping the car on the gravel road. His breath comes in bursts as though his chest will explode. His hands are clammy as they clutch the steering wheel, but he is determined not to crash. He drives as fast as he dares, wishing he had more experience.

Once Stan sees Paul obey his orders, he runs down the driveway, zigzagging between trees, and crouches in shadows until he reaches the cleared expanse of gravelled parking space, where the Ute is parked. He remains hidden while he scans the area, ignoring the drizzle. It's definitely the stolen Ute, but another car is also in the parking area. It's hidden by the bend in the driveway. He wonders if the escapees have reinforcements or if it's a friend. Stan surveys the terrain for clues, but the fog creeping in, obscures his view.

The laundry door opens a crack, and a dishevelled dark-haired man peers out into the drizzle. His body is bent at an odd angle, hidden behind the half-open door as if he's afraid. He stares at Stan, but doesn't react. Stan realises he's obscured by the mist. The door closes, and a bolt shoots home, loud in the otherwise silent space.

Stan remains crouched in observation mode, but after a few minutes his legs cramp. He must move. He's too old for this caper. How long before the police arrive? He glances at his watch. There isn't a police station within half an hour of this place, and even then it's only manned part-time by a single constable. If only he had a weapon.

He crosses the open parking area, running at a crouch, the gravel scrunching under his feet. His breathing is laboured, but he reaches the wall of the house, and leans his back flat against it, trying to catch his breath. Then he edges his way along the wall, and peers through the window into the dark laundry. It's empty.

The light from the hallway spills across the narrow room, highlighting an ironing board, a washing basket, the tumble dryer and washing machine, but little else. He tries the laundry door on the off chance, but it's definitely locked. The front doors are certain to be locked. He edges around the house making his way to the terrace.

In the car, Paul pulls up at the intersection of two country roads. On every side, fields roll away into the muted late afternoon light.

Elaine has the mobile pressed to her ear. She hangs up and says, 'they are sending the Special Emergency Response Team. I told them we would meet them here. The local police constable is also on his way.'

Paul says, 'Can I leave you and Abby here Gram. I'll go back and help Pops.'

'Don't be foolhardy Paul. You are not equipped to deal with criminals.'

'Neither is Pops. He'll need help.'

'We will wait until the police arrive. Your Grandfather knows what he's doing and will wait for the police. All he will do is gather intelligence, so that when they arrive, there'll be no waste of time.'

Paul slumps in his seat. He feels useless. It's his Mum and Dad in there. He sits forward and says, 'you don't understand Gram. I have to help. Mum knew this would happen. She needs us.' His gaze pleads with her.

Elaine holds out her hand. 'Give me the car keys.'

He passes the keys to her, bemused by the demand, and she drops them into her handbag and snaps it shut.

'You'll stay here Paul. No sense in putting another person in danger. Your Pops is experienced. He knows what to do, and he said for you to call the police. Just settle down until they arrive.'

Paul gets out the car and paces back and forth along the deserted road, oblivious to the drizzle, as he tries to get his frustration under control. Abby sits in the car, shocked into silence, crying quietly as she tries to remember prayers from her childhood. She says fragments she can remember under her breath so Gram won't hear her. Her Mum and Dad can't be in danger. She needs them.

Lights appear on the horizon, shafting into the sky as a four wheeled drive ascends the hill. Paul stops at the side of the road as the car draws up beside him. He recognises the local police officer although he can't remember his name. He's seen him in the village gym occasionally.

Elaine roles down her window. 'Constable Wilkes, I'm Elaine Fraser. I made the call. It's my daughter and son-in-law at the farm with my husband.'

Wilkes says, 'evening Mrs Fraser. I met your husband once.' He nods at Abby and Paul and says, 'SERTs on the way so all will be right once they arrive although it might be a while before they can get up here from Cairns. We can save time if I can get details.'

Wilkes pulls out a pen and a small note pad. Paul looks at him in amazement. Abby's stops crying to listen through her open window. Elaine opens her mouth to speak, but Abby interjects.

'This isn't a bloody car accident! What details? My parents are in mortal danger, and you want to take down details in your little notebook. What do you mean details?' Her voice shrills, 'our

167

statistics?'

Paul tries to remain calm, but his sister is right. 'We can't just stand around here talking! We have to help my parents and Pops.'

Elaine stretches out her hand. 'Constable, what do you mean SERT will be ages getting here from Cairns?'

'Well it's a two hour drive Mrs Fraser. The team will be called out, get their gear, then drive up here, two and a half hours would be the soonest they could get here I imagine.'

Abby voice shrills as she says, 'don't they have a helicopter?' She had imagined a scene from a movie where the helicopter rises, dark and menacingly, over the hill, with its spotlights blinding, pointing its bristling arsenal at the fugitives while loud hailers squawk orders to throw down their weapons.

'Right, well um, where was I? Yes – they might borrow a helicopter from EMQ—ah, Emergency Management Queensland that is, but it depends on how dire they consider the circumstances of the crime, and whether it's a crime in action, which is both serious and threatening to the public.'

'Well Constable you can be assured that this crime fits both those categories, so do you think you can persuade them to borrow the helicopter?'

'That's not my role Mrs Fraser. They will do what they do. They are the best we have you know, trained for every emergency. Now if I take down the details, I can radio them as they travel up here. It'll save time,' he adds once more as if to convince them.

'Radio the details!—What details?' Fury replaces fear as Abby hones her focus on Constable Wilkes. 'If anything happens to my parents, you will be responsible.'

'Abby, you are not helping.' Elaine says it more sharply than she intends. She knows Abby is worried and frightened, and it's just the way she copes.

Paul walks around to the driver's door of the car. 'Well I'm not hanging around for two hours while my parents are in danger. I'm going to help Pops.'

He looks so determined. It reminds Elaine of him as a little boy, stubborn and single-minded like his father. She watches his resolve fade as he remembers where the keys are, and he looks to Elaine pleadingly.

Gently she says, 'Paul, this is a job for professionals. Let's just give Constable Wilkes the details, and he can tell us the process. He'll know what we should do, and how the police will save your Mum and Dad and Pops.'

Paul hears the strain behind Elaine's calm exterior. It's her husband and her daughter that are in danger. Not only he and Abby are worried.

He sighs. 'Okay, sorry Gram.' He sinks into the car seat.

Abby hisses over the back of his seat. 'Do something Paul.'

He ignores her, and listens to Elaine as she outlines the facts she knows, along with names, addresses and phone numbers.

The constable's phone rings interrupting her flow. He listens then says, 'they're arriving within the next fifteen minute—in the helicopter. We need to organise lights to show them where it's safe to land.'

Constable Wilkes becomes a scurrying ball of authority as he orders Paul to move the car, and turn his car lights to shine on a place in the road, where he thinks the helicopter can land.

Three more police cars arrive from neighbouring villages, and night has fallen by the time the helicopter arrives. Its downdraft turns rain and mist into stinging pellets, and silences the din of the evening cicada song.

Elaine and Abby stand by the car, holding their skirts. Paul leans on the car roof, enthralled as it lands, and six men jump out carrying assault rifles.

Chris Zonda, loose limbed and in command of the

camouflaged unit, holds out a large well shaped hand to Elaine as he introduces himself. He looks worried but calm. He had been going off duty when the call came in, but when he heard Maggie was at the farmhouse, he insisted on taking charge himself.

His men busy themselves, transferring gear from the helicopter to the Constable's four by four. The pilot fiddles with his radio. Chris asks questions and listens attentively to Elaine's replies.

His deep voice casts a bubble of warm refuge around the little party standing in the headlights under the low drizzly sky. Abby smooths her shirt and tucks stray strands of hair behind her ears as she gazes at her newfound hero.

The headlights cast dark shadowed planes across the angles of his jaw and nose as he issues orders to the men. She knows now, her parents will be safe.

Two more police cars arrive and are deployed with the others to set up the perimeter. Then Chris climbs into the cab of the Constable's four by four with his men, and they take off down the road. The only people left behind with Elaine and the twins are Constable Wilkes and the helicopter pilot.

Abby gazes after Chris, feeling the chill of his departure as the mist closes behind the taillights, leaving the dark road empty. The helicopter lifts off into the night, but she barely notices the wind whipping her long hair across her face. She turns to her Gram. 'Paul's right, we need to follow them, they might need us.'

'No dear, they said to wait until Constable Wilkes gets the all clear.' Her Grandmother's will prevails and Abby throws herself into the back seat of the car, staring gloomily out the window. A moment later, she leans over to reach into the luggage space behind the back seat and scrabbles for her make-up bag.

19.

Revenge

Maggie sits at the head of the table with her head bowed. She is bathed in a pool of light from the overhead lamp. Her eyes are closed, and her hands clutch Tatjana's hand and Brendan's wrist.

With theatrical emphasis she throws back her head, and in a deep drawn-out tone says, 'oh Great Spirit we call on you to help this Mother waiting in the shadows. Let her pass through our earthly veil, so she may speak with her son one last time before eternity claims her. Cast your mantle of protection across this home to shield us from evil as you guide us in goodness.'

Joe stares in awe at his wife, hardly believing what he sees. Gone is the diminutive slip of femininity in shorts and inside-out tee-shirt. Instead the lamplight casts her shadow to loom across the room, its shade rising from the wall behind her chair to cover the ceiling. Bright tangled hair shines in halo above her shadowed body, her cheeks and forehead glow above the planes of her jaw. It's almost as if all that remains of his wife is a floating, disembodied head; as if her spirit is subsumed by caricature.

Tatjana's upper body sprawls across the table, her arm stretched across to grasp Brendan's wrist while her other hand clutches Maggie's. She stares wide eyed, hoping the séance is an act. The urge to make the sign of the cross is compelling, but she dare not remove her hand. Silently, she prays prayers from her childhood. *Hail Mary, full of Grace, blessed are thou, among women...* But she can't remember the rest of the words and repeats the same lines. She turns to look at Brigitte, but she can't move her head far enough around without losing Brendan's wrist.

From outside Julian wails. 'It's raining. Brendan, Brendan, it's raining, you bastard!'

Maggie's voice changes to that of an older woman with a broad Irish brogue. She croons a soft lullaby, the words indistinct. A chill damp breeze blows through the open door and swirls about the room, billowing curtains and setting off tinkling chimes.

Brendan drops the pistol and knife as his hands stretch-out. His face twists and he cries, 'Ó Ma Tá mé anseo le tú a!'

Maggie opens one eye. Bugger she hadn't bargained on another language.

Tatjana is immobile with indecision. Should she reach across the table to grab the pistol, and knife? The knife is the closest, but if she is not fast enough Brendan will still have the pistol, and she might ruin Maggie's plan.

She glances at Brigitte who frowns at her. She doesn't know what the frown means and looks toward Maggie, who appears to understand and nods. Without thinking further, she leaps up and grabs the knife. Brendan's arm swings around catching the side of her head. She staggers, her vision blurs, but she remains upright still clutching the knife, and blunders across the room.

She must get away. If she can make it around the house to the van, she can go for help. Her muscles pump as she slews out the open doors. The sound of gunfire galvanises her, and she dodges sideways, glancing behind to see if Brendan follows, but he is obscured from her line of sight. She runs on, looking over her shoulder and collides with Julian, still bound in his chair.

Together they topple over to skid across the paving, locked in twisted embrace. Another bullet whines past, centimetres above her head. The fall saved her, but now winded, she lies defeated, the knife lost from her grasp. Brendan steps out through the glass doors and lumbers towards her.

Stan crouches at the corner of the house. When Brendan first fired, he stopped and ducked behind the wall. Then he saw the young woman bolt out and collide with a man who appears to be tied to a chair. Who are these people? He watches Brendan come out of the house and sees the pistol in his outstretched hand.

Brendan sobs. 'Ye chased her away. I'm going to kill you, ye skankin' sleeveen. Ye chased me Ma away.' He walks up to the woman on the ground and points the pistol at her.

To Stan's surprise, another man runs out from the house, and weaves his way to stand swaying between the gunman, and the entangled couple on the ground.

Tatjana stares up at him, resigned to her fate like a doe in the jaws of a lion.

A grin spreads across Taylor's face, and he laughs as he kicks Julian's foot. 'You got your girl then pervert.' He kicks Julian again and turns to Brendan. 'Chill out Brendan. You're stoned mate. The bitch drugged us an' whatever you think is happening, isn't okay.'

Brendan's eyes bulge. 'No I saw her. The witch brought her here, I saw me Ma.' He nods vigorously, 'and that hoor,' he points at Tatjana, 'chased her away. I'm gonna kill her.'

'Who did you see mate?' Taylor's voice soothes. 'No one's here; just us, and we need to go. I heard a car. I reckon the Filth is coming.'

Brendan is beyond focusing on any risk to himself. All he wants is to talk to his Mother. 'No, she brought me Ma. She was going ta talk to me. I saw her.'

'Na.' Taylor clutches Brendan's forearms and looks into his crazed eyes. 'Get a grip Brendan. Your Ma was never here. You're stoned. The witch is lying to you.'

'No!' Brendan wrenches out of Taylor's grasp. 'You're trying to stop me talking to her.' He points the pistol.

Taylor is worried now. Brendan is out of control. 'Okay, your Ma was here, but if she came once she can come again. The witch can bring her back, but we need to get out of here.'

'No, not until I've spoken to me Ma. She doesn't have much time.'

Brendan thrusts out his chin, while his unsteady hand waves the pistol at Taylor's chest. He's forgotten his captives. He's forgotten everything except that this man is blocking him from helping his Ma.

The years fall away and Brendan stands in the hallway of the house he lived in as a small child. The Garda stands in the hallway barring his entry. He strains to see beyond, to where his mother lies on the cold stone kitchen floor. Someone needs to clean her, wipe the vomit from her mouth, make her warm, and put a pillow under her head.

He tries to thrust past, but the Garda puts a hand to his chest. Brendan peers around Taylor at the two tangled people on the tiles. 'Ma, are you all right, Ma?' Something is wrong. Why is his Ma tangled with his Pa? His Pa killed his Ma and the Garda won't let him pass.

He pulls the trigger. Taylor spins around as the bullet rips across his ribs, blowing a furrow through his left external oblique muscle. He staggers and falls off the terrace to land in the remnants of dinner dishes from last night's seduction.

Stan leaps up as Brendan fires and races along the length of the terrace, sprinting the distance as if a younger man, adrenalin fuelling his atrophied muscles. His bulk crashes against the blubbering Brendan. The pistol flies from his hand, to land with a clatter on the tiles. The two men, locked in embrace, slide across the terrace to join Taylor on the sodden lawn. Taylor staggers upright. Blood stains his clothes as he lurches back onto the terrace.

Inside Maggie cuts through the final strand of tape holding Joe. He leaps up and dashes outside just as Taylor bends to retrieve the pistol.

Joe's boot catches him in the face, sending him reeling backwards. As he lands, Taylor cracks the back of his head on the tiles and lies dazed, staring into the rain, disoriented, but conscious as blood seeps into puddles beneath him.

Joe picks up the pistol. He holds it in both hands pointing at Taylor. He has never in his life held a real weapon. His entire knowledge about guns is from toys he played with as a kid, and movies he has seen. He isn't sure how to use it, except he knows if he pulls the trigger it will fire just as it did with Brendan moments ago.

Brendan kicks out in desperate attempt to wiggle out from Stan's winded embrace. His boot catches Stan in the head, and he crawls away on all fours calling for his Ma.

Joe moves the pistol to point at Brendan, shouting at him to lie down on the ground. Stan hoists himself up and tackles Brendan again. Taylor tries to stand. Joe moves the pistol back. Christ, he needs help. Why is Maggie taking so long?

Inside Maggie cuts through the final strand of Brigitte's bonds using the Swiss Army knife she liberated from Joe's pocket when she cut him free. Then she runs outside with Brigitte. When she sees Joe with the pistol she stops.

The soft strains of jazz drift from the house. Mist swirls about the terrace lit by the lamplight spilling from the windows and doors. Joe stands legs apart, both hands pointing the pistol from one criminal to the other. Taylor lies on his back on the wet terrace. Brendan sprawls belly down in the grass, kicking to free himself from a man hanging onto his legs.

What's her father doing here? 'Dad?'

Julian shouts, 'Maggie, thank God. Cut me free, Maggie.' He giggles and sings bits of a Rod Stewart song. 'Oh, Maggie, I couldn't have tried any more. Just to save you from being alone, the morning sun, when it's in your face, really shows your age.'

'Maggie, take the gun,' Joe calls, shocking her from immobility.

'He's bleeding.' Maggie looks at Joe, her eyes round with shock. 'Did you kill him? Is he going to die? I'll get bandages and call an ambulance.' She turns to head into the house.

Joe shakes his head. 'I didn't shoot him. Maggie, come back. Fuck the bandages and take the gun.'

Maggie stops and looks back at Joe. She's afraid. She glances at Taylor lying on the ground. He's watching her. 'Joe he's going to do something.'

'Take the gun Maggie. I need to help Stan. Shoot the bastard if he tries anything.'

'I'm scared.' She walks back to Joe.

'I know Maggie honey, but you have to take the gun.' He places it in her hand, and points it at Taylor.

'Please, Joe. Look at his face. He's going to do something. I don't trust him... Joe.'

Brigitte takes the pistol from Maggie's hand. 'I'll hold the gun. I'll kill the Huhrensohn.' Her voice is menacing in its coldness.

Taylor starts laughing.

Brigitte steps closer to stand over him. 'What you laughing at Drecksau?'

'Ah Drecksau. My father would agree with you.'

'Shut your face, du arschgefickter Hurensohn!'

'My, my I think you and I may have attended the same education system.'

'Fick dich Arschloch. I'm not afraid to shoot you.'

'What; a wounded helpless man?'

'Fick deine Mutter.'

Taylor's face clouds. The reference to fucking his mother reclaims his drugged imagination.

Maggie comes out from the house clutching a length of tape, looped into a slipknot. Under her arm is a first aid box. 'I'll bandage him first to stop the bleeding.' She leans over to tend to his wounds. 'Stay still or you'll bleed to death.'

In LSD fuelled hallucination, Taylor sees his mother's face looming over him. The dark red lipstick on her pouting mouth darkens the age cracks leaking around her lips. The mouth opens into a yawning cavern from which blood flows. He throws up his arms to ward her off and screams in terror.

Maggie slips the loop of electrical tape around his arms and pulls the slip knot tight. 'We have to stop the bleeding, and phone for the police, and an ambulance,' she says to no one in particular.

She bandages him as best she can, then says to Brigitte, 'keep him covered with the gun. I'm not sure how good my knots are.'

Brigitte nods, keeping the pistol trained on Taylor and Maggie goes to help Tatjana. She lies huddled next to Julian, with her face hidden in her hands, as if she can't bear to see any more.

As Maggie bends to help her, Julian shouts, 'leave her and untie me Maggie. You have to help me first.'

Maggie ignores Julian and kneels beside Tatjana, stroking her wet hair. 'Come on, let's get you up and inside, out of the rain.'

Tatjana doesn't move and Maggie is worried. 'Are you hurt?' She runs her hands over Tatjana's back, but can't see any significant damage. Maggie grasps her shoulders and tries to turn her around, but Tatjana curls into a smaller ball.

On the lawn, Joe sits on Brendan's legs while Pops handcuffs his hands behind his back.

Brendan has stopped fighting and sobs. 'Me Ma you killed me Ma. Ye took her from me, Ma, Oh Ma.'

Joe is irritated with the man's crazy belief he's seen his dead mother. 'Your Ma's not here, you nutter. You're off your rocker. Get a grip.'

Pops says, 'thanks son, I didn't think I could hold him much longer. I'll need rope to tie this bastard's feet.'

'You'll find electrical tape in the sitting room. They used it on us.'

Pops raises his eyebrows, but says nothing as he goes inside to find the tape. Joe sits on Brendan and watches Maggie kneeling by Tatjana. He looks at his wife with new understanding and pride, before remorse surges in his throat, threatening to choke him. His gaze slides over to Brigitte. He brought them all into this.

Stan comes out holding the tape, and Joe clears his throat to focus on securing Brendan. Then he walks over to Brigitte and lays his hand on hers to take the pistol. 'I'm so sorry I brought you to this,' he says quietly.

She stares at him as if she has never seen him before, but surrenders the pistol. Then she goes over to Tatjana and squats beside Maggie. 'Leave her. I look after her.'

Maggie stands back and watches as Brigitte pulls Tatjana into her arms and holds her to her chest, murmuring into her hair. After a few minutes Brigitte coaxes Tatjana to stand up and go inside, out of the rain.

Maggie follows and as she passes Joe she says, 'I'll call the police and an ambulance.'

He nods and says, 'are you all right?'

'Yes,' her gaze drops from his scrutiny, and she hurries into the house.

His eyes sting and he squeezes them shut for a moment before once more focussing on keeping Taylor and Brendan under surveillance.

Julian shouts, 'hey what about me?'

No one pays any attention except Stan, who leaves Brendan babbling on the lawn to walk over to Joe. He nods at Julian. 'What about that one?'

'He can stay there for the moment. He's more trouble than he's worth.'

Stan raises his brow, 'is he linked to the crims?'

'No, he's a student... sorry, was a student. He's drugged.'

'Oh.' Stan frowns at Julian, but decides details can wait.

Joe says, 'you timed your entry perfectly. How did you know?'

Stan scratches his chin. 'I didn't really. We drove up the driveway and things looked amiss. I just smelled rats, and then I saw the vehicle they stole so I sent the kids and Elaine for help while I scouted around. When the firearm went off, I thought I had better do something before one of you ended-up dead. Elaine will have called the police by now. They should be here any minute. Will you be all right out here by yourself if I go in and give them a ring?'

'Yeah. I don't think either of these two, are going anywhere.' Joe dashes rain from his eyes. 'But if you can ask them to hurry, that'd be good.'

Stan goes inside, and Joe watches Taylor. Brendan is trussed up and babbling to his mother. He seems less of a danger than Taylor whose legs are still free. He should have asked Stan to tie him up properly before he went into the house. The tape Maggie tied around his arms looks loose, but the guy appears lost in a bizarre hallucination of his own. He's cringing and mumbling and licking his lips as if he's in the throes of his own demons. Jesus, what did Maggie give them?

20.

Restitution

'Police! Drop the weapon.' A commanding voice rings across the lawn.

Joe spins around, the pistol still pointing straight out in front of him. 'Thank God. Where are you?' He peers into the dark shadows beyond the pool of light from the house.

The voice becomes more urgent. 'Drop the weapon, now!'

Joe looks at the pistol in his hand with surprise, and then he kneels to put it down on the terrace tiles. He's careful because the last thing he wants is the bloody thing to go off accidentally.

'Step away from the weapon and put your hands behind your head.'

Joe stands up and steps away.

Taylor struggles from his ties and gropes for the pistol. Joe places his boot on Taylor's hand causing the wounded man to cry out.

The disembodied voice shouts again. 'Step away.'

Joe is not sure what to do. He looks down at Taylor, whose hand now clutches the pistol.

Pops comes out the door behind him. 'You're a bit bloody late young Christopher. That's my son-in-law you have in your sights. The crims are there and over there.' He points to Taylor, and then to Brendan crooning to himself on the lawn.

For a moment, only the noise of night insects and frogs disturb the quiet. Then a dark shape materialises from the bushes to flit across the garden, followed by several more.

Stan walks over to Taylor and kicks his wounded flank. Taylor screams and tries to pull his hand out from Joe's boot. It's enough distraction for Stan to lean over and scoop up the pistol.

Joe remains still, with his hands behind his head, while three men in camouflage uniforms and helmets take up positions around the terrace covering them with assault rifles. Other shadows flit past and disappear around the house.

The man, whose commands Joe obeyed, walks across the lawn and steps up onto the terrace. His eyes flick uncertainly to Stan, who stands next to Joe, grinning. He's enjoying himself at Chris's expense.

Chris nods at Stan and says to Joe, 'you can put your hands down now sir.'

With relief Joe lowers his arms. Nausea wells up from his gut and his muscles shake. 'I think I might need to sit down,' he glances at Stan apologetically.

Chris asks, 'are there others here?'

'My daughter and two other women.'

'Check it out,' Chris says and two men disappear into the house.

Stan says, 'Chris, meet my son-in-law, Dr. Joe Williams. He saved the day here and captured your crims for you.' Pride fills Stan's voice.

'No.' Joe shakes his head. 'It was Maggie. I did nothing. My wife is a bloody miracle…and you Stan. If you hadn't intervened when you did, someone would be dead now.' Joe's legs shake and his arms tremble. 'I have to find Maggie.'

At that moment a police officer walks through the door with Maggie, Brigitte and Tatjana in front of him. 'Found three more, sir,' he says to Chris. 'This one says she is Mrs Williams, owner of the house. These are Tatjana and Brigitte somebody or other. I can't pronounce their surnames.' He grins at the German backpackers. 'They claim to be tourists. It's their van and bag in the driveway. She,' he indicates Maggie, 'says she called triple zero, and an ambulance is on its way.'

Chris stares at Maggie's battered face, and loses his composure. 'Christ, are you okay?'

She drops her eyes, embarrassed at him seeing her in such a mess, and nods her head. 'I'm okay.'

He continues staring at her as an image bubbles into his mind. For the last month, he's felt he knew her from somewhere and now he knows from where. She is the terrified young woman in the bank, with the blonde ponytail, who haunts his dreams.

Joe walks over without a word and puts his arms around her. Maggie buries her face in his chest and they stand holding each other.

She can feel his muscles shake as exhaustion claims him, and says, 'are you all right?'

'Mm,' he rests his cheek on the top of her head and closes his eyes.

Chris walks away, his hand cupped around a microphone poking out from his helmet as he speaks into it. When he returns he passes Julian and says, 'who's this?'

Julian lies on his side, watching every move, wondering if he is likely to be in trouble or if he can turn the situation to his advantage. The drugs addle his thinking, but he tries to focus so he can work out how to respond. It's clear none of them will support him despite the fact that they have lured him into such a risky situation. He's the injured party in all this. Nobody said the farm stay would be dangerous. They will have to pay.

Maggie lifts her head and says, 'he's our house sitter, Julian Borodin, an exchange student from America.'

'Julian Borodin the third please, and I'm gonna sue your ass if you don't get me out of here quick smart,' Julian farts and giggles.

Chris looks at Stan's disgusted face. 'What's with him?'

Stan says, 'he's been using drugs apparently.'

Brigitte spits at him. 'He's a pervert.'

Chris looks confused and says to Stan. 'Can we cut him lose?'

Stan says, 'you'll have to ask Joe.'

Joe lifts his head from Maggie's and says wearily. 'He is our house sitter and he is drugged.' His gaze settles on her face. 'I suppose we should let them help him, what do you think Maggie?' He looks into his wife's eyes. 'Shall we forgive and forget?'

Maggie drops her gaze. 'Yes. He's a perverted drop-kick, but I suppose...' She buries her face in Joe's shirtfront, and he holds her tighter.

Chris nods to one of the men covering them. The man lowers his weapon and walks over to cut Julian's ties. He wrinkles his nose at the smell.

Julian stands up swaying until a police officer grabs his arm to steady him, but he shakes off the man and stalks towards the house, his legs moving sideways. 'I need a shower,' he says haughtily.

He passes Maggie and Joe, and then at the last minute, diverts to where Taylor still lies on the ground. Before the officer escorting him is aware of his intentions, Julian aims a kick at Taylor's groin, but misses his target and stumbles against the wall.

'Oi!' The police officer grabs him and pushes him towards the sliding doors. Julian trips over the step, but regains his balance and walks into the house.

Chris watches in consternation. He's not come across anything like this. He glances at Maggie and Joe. 'Perhaps we can go inside, out of the rain and you can explain what happened here.' He gestures for his men to see to Brendan and Taylor.

Stan follows. 'I'd like to ring and let Elaine, and the kids know things are okay here. If it's all right with you young Chris, I'll tell them they can come back to...'

He's interrupted by a curdled scream from inside the house. Chris curses and runs into the sitting room. The others follow.

Julian comes through the door shouting, 'it's not my shit. I didn't do it. It was like that when I got there.'

The officer follows him and says, 'whose shit is it then?'

Julian tries to push past the officer. 'I'll use the master bathroom.'

He blocks Julian's way. 'Just a minute mate.' He speaks to Chris in a low voice.

A moment later, a look of disgust crosses Chris's face and he turns to Maggie. 'I'm sorry, but I think something is wrong with your house sitter. Apparently, he's made a mess all over the bathroom.'

Tatjana's face lights up. It's the first time since she arrived in this house she has been able to smile, and now she can feel laughter gurgling up inside her as Julian protests his innocence. Brigitte sees the mirth in her face and puts her arm around her. The two German women stand arm in arm and laugh.

Chris watches with concern. This looks to him like a shock reaction. The distant sound of an ambulance siren brings him back to the business at hand. 'Make him clean up the mess and himself,' he says to the officer. 'He's not using the master bathroom.' He turns to Joe. 'You will need to dry off too sir, and then perhaps you will feel up to providing a statement?'

Out on the farm road, Paul drives behind the ambulance with Elaine beside him. Constable Wilkes and Abby are in the back seat. The noise of the ambulance fills Abby with anticipation. Her parents and Pops are safe. Her hero has saved them. Chris Zonda. She repeats his name in her mind as she presses her forehead against the cool window pane.

Paul pulls up in the driveway behind the ambulance. Someone has moved the van and picked up the backpack. A police officer dressed in camouflage, his assault rifle cradled in one arm, holds open the laundry door for the ambulance officers. Paul and Elaine follow, but Abby stands in the driveway trying to straighten her clothing and smooth her hair.

When she enters the sitting room, she stares in shock at the mess. She has never before seen their house so untidy. Dirty plates with congealed curry lie about the room. Chairs are tipped over or out of place, festooned by what looks like lengths of the electric tape Dad sometimes uses for fencing cattle. Jazz plays incongruously in the background and lights blaze, giving a hard edge to the chaos.

The room is full of dishevelled looking people, including her parents, and the German backpackers she and Paul met at the party in Townsville. What are they doing here? Just like Paul not to tell her. She sees him with his arms around Mum and Dad, and she bursts into tears. She runs to them, and Joe puts his weary arm around her, hushing her sobbing as he strokes her hair.

Elaine examines Maggie and Joe's injuries. 'They'll heal,' she says and goes in search of towels. Stan goes outside to the terrace and watches the ambulance officers' staunch Taylor's bleeding. They lift him onto a stretcher and then tend to Brendan.

Paul dashes the back of his hand across his face and glances across the room. To his astonishment, Tatjana and Brigitte are standing near the dining table. He walks over to them. 'What are you doing here?' His voice is young and uncertain, and he clears it to smile at Tatjana, but she doesn't return his greeting.

A police officer walks up and says, 'excuse me mate, I need to get statements. Ladies we can sit down here, please.' He indicates the chairs used only forty minutes before in mock séance.

Tatjana looks nervously at the chair. Brigitte takes her hand and they sit side by side, thighs touching as they wait for the police officer. They ignore Paul. He hovers, but doesn't leave. After a moment he pulls up another chair. No one objects, so he sits down to listen. He wants to hear this.

Elaine brings Joe and Maggie towels, which she drapes over their shoulders. Chris suggests they sit down on the sofa.

Stan returns, 'the helicopter is on its way. I'll organise lighting, if you are okay with that son?'

Chris nods. 'Thanks mate.' He turns back to Maggie and Joe. He recognises the exhaustion in both their faces as he pulls up a chair to talk to them. Abby sits down on the sofa next to her parents. She clutches her mother's arm, and gazes at Chris.

Elaine says, 'do you need me to do anything?'

He looks at her kindly. 'Perhaps you could make sweet tea. They're going to need it.' His deep voice casts an obliging spell as he looks at Abby. 'You might help your Grandmother.'

Abby surprises Joe by jumping up to do his bidding. As she follows Elaine to the door, Julian returns. His hair is still wet from the shower and he wears clean clothes. He leers at her as she passes and slides his hand around her waist.

Maggie leaps up from the couch. 'Don't touch her you bastard. I'll kill you if you touch her.'

Chris stands up, ready to act, but unsure of the circumstances. Joe remains seated, unable to muster the strength to get up, but he smiles as he watches his brave wife defend their daughter.

To Elaine's consternation, Julian winks at her before weaving across the room to help himself to brandy from the liquor cabinet.

Chris glances down at Joe. 'Are you certain that man is your house sitter?'

'Yes,' says Joe, the weariness in his voice barely held in check. 'He was, but never again.'

Abby flees to the safety of the kitchen. Elaine follows her out, and when they are out of Julian's reach Maggie sinks down on the sofa. Joe slides his arm around her shoulders and pulls her close, his face in her hair.

An ambulance officer and a policeman carry in a sedated

Brendan on a stretcher, followed by a second stretcher with Taylor strapped to it. Everyone in the room stops talking and watches. The police officer jerks his head at Chris, who looks apologetically at Maggie and Joe, and goes over to the stretchers.

After speaking with the policeman, Chris returns to Maggie. 'We need to get them out of the rain until the chopper gets here. We'll medivac them to Cairns Base hospital and the chopper will come back for us. They want to know if your cuts and bruises need attention.' She shakes her head. When he sits down again he says. 'Don't worry; they'll be doing a long stretch for this.'

For the first time in years, Maggie doesn't feel worried. Her worst fears materialised, she met them head on, and now she is the victor. Lightness fills her chest, and she gazes into Joe's worried eyes, trying to convey the hope she has for the future. She turns back to Chris. 'Can you give us a minute?'

He nods, and gets up to walk over to Julian, and takes the glass from his hand. 'You've had enough, mate.'

Julian says, 'hey.'

Maggie looks up, a smile on her face.

Chris says, 'you can go down with the other two in the chopper so the hospital can pump your stomach. He summons one of his men over and gives them instructions.

Julian looks bewildered. 'You can't do that. I haven't done anything.'

Chris glances over to Maggie then back to the officer. 'Arrest him for obstruction or something if he gives you any grief.'

He walks over to the dining table where he stands with his hands on the back of Tatjana's chair, and listens to Brigitte give a halting account of how they came to be at the house.

Paul also listens to Brigitte's story, and knows she is lying. But why lie? Perhaps she is still confused. They told him last week they were leaving Townsville yesterday morning, not today. So where were they last night? Besides, that bit about them finding his Dad lost in the forest is bullshit. His Dad knows the forest well, and he would never go into it without a sat nav. He remains silent and glances across the room to where Julian sits at the desk, wondering if he is somehow mixed up in the backpackers' lies.

Outside, a noise grows to a deafening roar, drowning out all other sound. Tatjana shrinks back, and Brigitte hovers, ready to bolt. Julian looks at the ceiling in terror.

Chris says, 'it's okay, it's just the helicopter.'

The chopper lands on the lawn in the lit front garden. Joe closes his eyes as the noisy hub-hub quietens to silence. Pops comes in through the glass doors and sits on a chair.

When he tackled Brendon, he pulled a tendon in his thigh and cracked his knee on the concrete, but otherwise he feels in remarkably good shape. Perhaps it's just the remnants of adrenalin, but he has a moment of wistful regret he has retired.

He gazes across the room to where Chris stands with the German girls. The dark one looks defiant, but scared at the same time. From what he saw, she is a brave and loyal friend to the blonde one. Stan values loyalty and inclines his head at her as she looks across the room to him.

She doesn't make any sign she's noticed, but he knows she's seen him and looks bolstered by his approval. He glances across to his grandson. The kid looks agitated. Stan wonders what that's about, but there will be plenty of time later to winkle out the details.

Elaine comes in with Abby carrying a tea tray. He looks at his wife fondly. She's always so practical; when in doubt make tea and tidy up things. Maggie gets her obsessive tidiness from her mother.

Elaine hands Maggie and Joe a cup of tea each, and Abby carries one over to Chris, who hands it to the blonde German girl.

Abby glares and walks away, her neck turning a mottled red.

As she passes him, Stan says, 'I'll have a cup of coffee young Abby.' She nods, but doesn't meet his gaze and walks out the door towards the kitchen. Stan sighs.

Elaine bustles about collecting plates and cutlery, stacking them on the trolley to wheel into the kitchen. Maggie gets up to help her. 'We will have to get rid of the curry. It's drugged.'

Elaine raises an eyebrow, but Joe interrupts before she can reply. The sweet tea has revived him and he gets up off the sofa to take Maggie's hand. 'Leave it.' Then he looks at Elaine and says, 'I'll be in the shower with my wife for a while.'

Maggie casts a self-conscious glance at her mother as she follows Joe out the room. From across the room, Chris watches her leave, before turning his attention back to the job at hand.

21.

Rebirth

Three months later…

'You'll like Melbourne Maggie.' Joe holds her loosely around the waist and looks into her eyes. 'I know you will. It's a great city, but if you try it and hate it, I promise we can come back. It's not like we're selling up, just trying something new for a while. When we're settled, the kids can transfer. It'll be an experience for them too, and we can come back here on holiday.' He looks out the window. 'I'll miss the view and the forest though.'

'I don't know how you can stand the forest anymore. If I was lost in it all night, I think I would die.'

Joe lets her go and turns to a pile of flat-pack boxes lying on the sitting room floor. 'No you wouldn't. Look what you've been through and survived.'

A week after the night Taylor and Brendan were arrested Stan had taken Paul down to Cairns, where Chris Zonda showed him around the SERT headquarters. He told Stan about the robbery in Sydney, adding if Maggie was anxious, it was probably due to post traumatic stress. This latest incident wouldn't help, and she should see someone. He said he'd seen a lot of it in his career, mostly with police officers. Stan had reported the conversation to Joe, but Maggie said she was all right now.

Joe glances at his wife, searching her face for signs of the old anxiety. 'Are you still afraid the bank robbers will find you?'

'No, not anymore. Chris said he rang up the New South Wales police to find out if they were ever caught. He said one of the robbers is in jail for murder. That's how they caught him. Apparently, he shot someone in a hold up, killed him, and he won't be out for a very long time. The other one got stabbed in a street fight and died. Only one of them has never been caught, but I don't think he even looked in my direction, so he won't recognise me. He was older than the other two, so with any luck he's also dead now.'

'When did you see Chris?' Jealousy flares, and he tries to keep it from showing, but Maggie is gazing out the window.

'At the final class last week. The parents put on a farewell at the pub to say goodbye. I'll miss them... the kids, that is. I loved teaching them.'

'That's the most bizarre coincidence, you and he being in the same bank.'

'It wasn't a coincidence.'

Joe sighs. 'Okay, sorry.'

My grandmother...

'Yeah, I know honey. Let's get on with it shall we. The packers will be here next week, and we need to sort out what we want to keep out, otherwise they'll pack the lot.'

'Joe...'

'Mmm.'

'I think when we get to Melbourne I'd like to try to get into Uni. Do you think I can?'

Surprised, Joe turns to look at her. 'Where did this come from?'

'I've been thinking about it for a while?'

'What do you want to study?'

'Teaching. If I can get a degree in teaching perhaps I can teach drama and dance somewhere.' Her eyes look anxious as she turns to look into his face. 'Is that a dumb idea?'

He smiles at her. 'No Mags, it's a damn fine idea. What a switch around. I'll be an unemployed musician, and you'll be at Uni. It's a great idea. If I can't find a job, I might join you, and then you can teach dance, and I can teach music. Hey, we can start our own academy.'

She bites her lip. 'I don't know if I'm clever enough…'

'Yeah, sure you are. Jesus, I reckon you're the one with the brains in this family. I would never have thought of what you did to those bastards, or been able to carry it off.'

Maggie frowns, but Joe doesn't notice and carries on speaking. 'It's just lucky you found those drugs in Julian's soap bag. Who would have thought the bloke was a drug addict. How did you figure it out?'

Maggie drops her gaze and changes the subject. 'Joe, are we going to go through your parents' trunk?'

His face clouds and he stares at his feet, silent for a moment. Then he says. 'You're right. I have to do it eventually. I'll do it right now. I've been putting it off long enough.' He turns to look at her with a wry smile. 'You're not only clever, but brave too. Come on, I need your courage.' He picks up a box.

'You want me to help?'

'Of course. I'm not sure I can do it by myself. If you take the stuff out, I'll go through it, and decide what we should keep and what should go.' He takes her in his arms again. 'I love you Maggie, you know that don't you. I know I've taken you for granted, but all that's changed now.'

She gazes into his eyes, and tiptoes to kiss him. 'I know Joe. I love you too. I was so scared I'd lose you, but it'll be fine. This is like a new start. We can make the trip to Melbourne like a honeymoon.'

He kisses her. Her lips are soft and giving under his, and he's surprised at his body's immediate response.

'Hey,' Maggie says as he unzips her skirt. 'Someone will see us. The doors are wide open.'

Joe mutters into her neck. 'There's no one about for miles.'

Maggie giggles as Joe pushes her back towards the sofa,

making growling noises as he drops her skirt to the floor, and pulls her tee-shirt over her head.

The sound of wheels scrunching on gravel distracts him. 'Shit.' He can feel the panic rising as he pulls up his jeans and straightens his shirt.

Maggie stands up and with a sly look says, 'I'll go and see who's here, shall I?'

'Jesus, Maggie, you're naked.'

She laughs at the shocked look on his face, and picks up her clothes, 'I'll see you in the bedroom.'

As Joe walks to the front door, shaking his head and smiling, she runs down the corridor in the other direction. A few minutes later, he returns. 'It was just the man to read the metre. Where were we?' He crawls across the bed to where Maggie lies posing naked and pouting.

A minute later, he remembers she prefers privacy and asks, 'do you want me to close the curtains?'

She tilts her head to look at him from under her lashes. 'No, why change the habits of a lifetime. I'm adopting your attitude. I refuse to worry about things that are unlikely to happen, like people turning up at inopportune moments.'

Joe winces. 'Okay touché.' He leans forward to kiss her.

*

An hour later they stand in the garage looking at the trunk. Maggie glances at his mouth set in a bloodless line. 'What is it Joe?'

He shakes his head staring at the tin trunk. 'My father made this you know. He was always good with his hands. Well, I say he made it, but really he bought two old tin trunks and welded them together, then lined it. I remember him doing it. I was just a kid, but it was one of the few good memories I have. He showed me how to use a saw.'

Maggie's brow furrows. 'Why are you so, um…so reluctant then?'

He glances at her and back to the trunk, but remains silent.

'Tell me. Is it because…'

'Leave it Mags.'

'Joe, it's been eighteen years since he died, nearly as long as we've been here. If he hadn't left that money, we would still be struggling to make ends meet in Sydney.'

'That's just it, isn't it?'

'What, I don't get it.'

He sighs, and turns to look at her. She gazes into his face. A muscle twitches in his jaw, and he takes a breath. 'Okay, no more secrets.'

Maggie feels her stomach flutter. Does she want to hear it? She stares up at her husband's face, etching every detail into her mind. 'What secrets?'

He takes a deep breath. 'I'm afraid I'll find out something I'd rather not know.'

'I don't understand.'

Joe turns away. 'My father died a rich man. How is that possible? He was a middle ranking public servant all his life, working in a department that over-sighted environment and planning. When he died, I worried about Mum meeting the mortgage payments, but I found out the house was in their names and fully paid. I couldn't find out how.'

Maggie lets the air out of her lungs. Is that all, but she says, 'I'm not sure what that means.'

He turns back and grasps her arms. 'He was dealing with developers. Don't you see, it means he might have been taking back-handers. The house was probably a *gift*.' He drops her wrists to make speech marks in the air.

'Oh.' Maggie's eyes shine green in the yellow light from the panel door Perspex as the full implication settles in her mind.

'You see? How can I live with it if I find out my father was a crook. I knew he suffered PTSD from his conscription in Vietnam, and I put most of his weird behaviour down to that, but what if it wasn't?'

Maggie bites her lip, surely not. She met Max and Beth. They were just Mr and Mrs Average in suburban Melbourne. Joe is being melodramatic. 'Maybe he was just really clever with investments. You know my dad would have checked out your family before we got married. He's always the policeman and suspects everyone. He would never have let me marry you if there was the slightest whiff of corruption in your family.' She smiles, and shrugs. 'It isn't a big deal. Come on, I bet we find nothing, but old photos and stuff.'

He takes another deep breath, relieved that he's shared his fear. 'You're right.' He's letting his imagination run riot.'

She smiles, and in an attempt to lighten the atmosphere, she mimics Joe, 'let's just look at the facts, shall we?'

He pulls his bottom lip. 'Okay.' He stands back and makes a gesture towards the trunk. 'After you.'

'You want me to open it?'

'Yeah, I reckon I do.'

She hesitates and looks into his eyes. 'You aren't tricking me are you? Is something going to jump out like a jack-in-a-box?'

'Tch,' he sucks his tongue off his palate. 'You don't really think I would do that.'

'Hmm.' She unhooks the latch and lifts the lid. It's heavy and he helps her. Tissue paper lifts with the breeze, to reveal a cream coloured gown in a plastic sheaf. 'Oh, it's beautiful.' She glances up and sees Joe's eyes are moist.

'My mother's wedding gown.' He lifts it from the trunk and looks about for somewhere to lay it.

'Hold on. I'll get something to put things on.' Maggie goes over to the other side of the garage and drags out a folding table. When it's set, Joe lays the plastic sheaf on it.

'Do you want to take it out and look at it?' He imagines it's a thing women like to do.

'Later. We'll take it inside. It shouldn't be in the garage anyway. It's amazing it's not mouldy or eaten by insects.'

'The trunk's lined with camphor.'

'Is that what the smell is?' Maggie wrinkles her nose. 'Oh look at this little dress.'

'My christening gown.'

'It's gorgeous. I bet you were such a cute baby.'

'Come on, we'll be here all day at this rate.'

'Photo albums—I told you that's all we'd find.' She opens the cover. 'Oh cute. I don't think I've seen your baby photos.'

'I got this far last time, but was side-tracked browsing through them. Can it wait?'

'Right.' she says placing the album on the table. 'We'll leave the distractions till last.' She lifts album after album, handing each one to him to pile on the table next to the others. Under the albums, several shoe boxes line the base of the trunk.

Joe raises his eyebrows. 'I never got this far.' He lifts the lid off the first box. It's full of papers. He hands it to Maggie. 'I can't look.'

She riffles through the top papers. 'They are just old invoices and boring stuff. There's nothing here Joe.'

Two more boxes with papers and letters follow. The next box is heavier and tied with string. It's full of jewellery.

'Crikey, are they your Mum's?' Maggie picks up a string of pearls. 'Wow, do you reckon these are real?'

He shrugs. 'I don't recall my Mum wearing much jewellery, except her wedding rings. She had some nice broaches too, if I recall, and maybe earrings, but I don't remember these. Oh shit you don't think…'

'Joe, stop imagining the worst. It's probably nothing. Maybe she inherited this stuff. Look this box has broaches and wedding rings, just as you said…oh, and letters.' Maggie pulls one of the letters from its envelope. 'It's from you.' She scans the first lines. 'Look, it's when you told her we were getting married. How lovely, she kept your letters.'

Joe's eyes burn as he takes the box from Maggie and puts it on the table. 'What's in the next one?' He clears the gravel from his throat.

Maggie opens another and looks puzzled. 'What is it?'

Joe takes the box and inhales. 'Christ, they're magazines.' He picks up the top one and looks at it. 'It's full of bullets.' Joe stares at the contents trying to work out what his father was doing with magazines and bullets. With relief he realises they must be a souvenir from his time in Vietnam.' He lays it back in the box and places them on the table. 'He would have owned these before the gun buyback laws.'

Maggie leans over the trunk. Four boxes remain. As she lifts the first she knows by its weight it contains the same. She lifts them out one by one and opens them, then hands them to Joe. 'That's a lot of souvenirs. 'Maybe your dad belonged to a gun club.'

Joe shakes his head, laying each box on the table. 'We'll have to hand them into the police I suppose.'

'Is it illegal to have bullets?'

'I don't know, but automatic weapons are illegal, and these look like they could belong to an illegal firearm. Not that I am any kind of expert. Come on, what's in the last box?'

'Maggie lifts it. 'Oh it's light.' She opens it to find a solitary tweed cap.

Joe takes it out and puts it on his head, cocking a pose and winking at Maggie.

She feels a chill rush across her shoulders. 'Take it off Joe.'

'Why, don't you fancy me in a shooting hat?'

Maggie shakes her head. It gives her a bad feeling although she isn't sure why. She snatches it off and throws it to the table. In an effort to make light of her reaction she turns away to gaze into the trunk. 'Well that's it. Looks like you were worried for nothing. Your Dad was an honest man, and only a tiny bit weird, keeping all these bullets.' She smiles, but Joe is staring at the trunk. 'What is it?'

For a moment he's silent then he says, 'the floor of the trunk is half the depth inside as out. Look.' He bends over and lays his hands flat on the wooden panelling at the base of the trunk. Screws either side hold it in place. He crosses the garage to retrieve a screw driver from his tool kit. As he unscrews one end, the ply board tilts.

He unscrews the remaining screws and lifts the board. Maggie catches her breath. A camouflage bag sits alongside another sports bag. Joe lifts out the camouflage bag. 'This might be Dad's old army gear.'

He unzips it, and inside lies a rifle wrapped in oil cloth. 'Holy shit! This is definitely an illegal weapon.' He lifts the AK 47 from its bag. 'Dad must have owned this before the buyback laws. It's probably more loot from Vietnam. Pity we didn't know about it when those rat-faced criminals were here.' He stops and a worried frown creases his forehead. 'Jesus, I hope the cops believe we didn't know it was here.'

Maggie's eyes are huge. She whispers. 'Joe I'm scared. Put it back. I don't want to see anymore.'

'It's all right honey. It's not loaded.'

He unzips the other bag and pulls out a black tee-shirt. As he shakes it, a black cloth falls onto the floor. Maggie's fist blocks her cry as she sees the howling jackal above a looping signature on the front of the tee-shirt. Very slowly as if mesmerized, she bends to retrieve the black bandanna. A muzzle-full of sharp canine teeth grins back at her.

'Jesus, Dad must have been a Bikie at some stage. I never heard about that saga in his life, but I guess a lot of Vietnam vets were, weren't they?' He's grinning at Maggie. 'Will you still love me if I'm the son of a bad-assed Bikie?' He glances down and strokes the rifle.

With anguished eyes she stares at her husband who is engrossed in examining the weapon. She can't tell him. It will destroy him. She can't let the kids know, their trust account is tainted. They are all living on stolen money.

Did Max know he ruined her life? Is that why he set up the kids' trust account and left that sympathy card? How can she live with herself? But this stuff can't end up in the hands of the police.

At least now she knows where the third robber is, and she never again has to fear any of them. No, but now she has another problem.

'Joe we have to bury this.'

He looks up at her. 'We should hand the rifle and magazines in to the police.'

'No Joe, trust me. I have a bad feeling. We have to bury it and pretend it never existed.'

He opens his mouth to argue, then remembers the other premonitions he dismissed. Does it matter if they bury it or hand it in to the authorities? No one knows it exists anyway, and he can't let her down again.

'Okay honey, we'll bury it.' He sighs. At least there is no incriminating evidence of corruption in the trunk. Maybe his father was on the straight and narrow after all. He turns to his wife. 'I don't know why I waited so long to go through it. It's a relief to know the old man wasn't corrupt, just as you said, he must have been a good investor.' He reaches over and takes her hand. 'I'm glad we did it together, thank you.'

She stares at the trunk as her dilemma stretches unresolved into the yawning chasm of infinity.

The End

Also by Gillian Long

Dying Days

ISBN: 978-0-9942671-1-5

A mystery about finding
Family, Love and Redemption
in a dying country.

It's the end of Mugabe's reign. Factions jockey for power. The scene is set for civil war. Matt Reid, an ex British Special Forces soldier, arrives in Australia in search of his biological father. He meets Alan Fletcher, a retired war correspondent, whose story about the disappearance of a Rhodesian SAS soldier in 1980 sends Matt off to Zimbabwe on a mission to find the truth. What he doesn't plan is to become a person of interest to a paranoid secret police or to uncover plots of treachery and revenge and a half century old family feud.

Watershed

ISBN: 978-0-9942671-4-6

A thriller about
the insidiousness of political corruption,
the dangers of social injustice, the fragility of democracy,
and the power of family, as one man prepares to abandon all he believes
in to save the woman he loves.

It's the end of the 2020s and Australia struggles under tyranny. The economy has collapsed as terrorism escalates. Conscript Blake Lincoln returns from an endless Middle East war, wounded and a National hero. When he meets Charlotte all he wants is to forget the war and have his old life back. Instead, he uncovers secrets that will blow the government apart. Watershed is set in Brisbane, Sydney, and Canberra. It takes in the vast wilderness of Cape York, and the raw beauty of the Kimberly, with flashbacks to war torn Baghdad.

https://gillianlong.wordpress.com

www.ingramcontent.com/pod-product-compliance
Lightning Source LLC
Chambersburg PA
CBHW050323200626
46810CB00022B/1189